Zebra Crossings

Zebra Crossings

Tales from the shaman's record

Peter Merrington

JACANA

The following stories were published in earlier versions: 'The Purple Panama', which won the Thomas Pringle Prize for 1996, in *New Contrast* 22,3, September 1994; 'Elephant's Breath' in *Senses of Culture: South African Culture Studies*, edited by Sarah Nuttall and Cheryl-Ann Michael, Oxford University Press, Cape Town, 2000; 'Khaki and Scarlet' in *A Is for Ancestors*, Caine Prize anthology, Jacana, Johannesburg, 2004; and 'Sage Green' in *Under Construction: 'Race' and Identity in South Africa Today*, edited by Natasha Distiller and Melissa Steyn, Heinemann, Johannesburg, 2004.

I acknowledge the assistance of the British Council/University of Lancaster 'Crossing Borders' project in the writing of this book, and the valued eye of my wonderful editor, Priscilla Hall.

First published by Jacana Media (Pty) Ltd in 2008
10 Orange Street
Sunnyside
Auckland Park 2092
South Africa
+2711 628 3200
www.jacana.co.za

ISBN 978-1-77009-542-7
Cover design by miss sweden
Set in Sabon 11/15pt
Printed by CTP Book Printers
Job No. 000619

See a complete list of Jacana titles at www.jacana.co.za

CONTENTS

THE WINE-DARK SEA

Far beyond the farthest end of the Tsitsikamma, the land runs down to the sea in wide stretches of fynbos and reed. This is the alluvial plain of the Gamtoos, Kouga and Van Staden's Rivers, the start of the Eastern Cape proper. It is alkaline country with birdlife and with small amphibians. Farmers keep fat sheep, or plant buchu for its value in the perfume industry. For all its richness it is a lonely tract with sparse tiny settlements of shepherds and gatherers and their ragged families. The farms on which they live are broad, though towards the more salty land at the coast there are smallholdings, the place of bywoners who live partly from their sheep and partly from the fishing. They have small *skuits*, rowing boats, sometimes with outboard motors, and they go out after crayfish in season, and the perlemoen, and the harder and the snoek. Their houses are remote. They live in isolation, willing or enforced.

One such house, slightly larger than the others, stood empty for forty years. Not quite a ruin, it stank of mouldy woodwork. The ceiling boards were sagging. The windows had all long lost their glass. The floorboards were rotten. A solid house, nonetheless, built up foursquare on high foundations, with a narrow steep flight of cement steps up to the kitchen door at the rear, a wider flight to the stoep that faced the sea. Solid enough to stand for decades more, although the tin roof was rusting through from the salt sea wind, and one day the trusses might fall.

Here a lone archaeologist had taken quarters, along with the swallows that nested under the roof, the wasps in places where mortar had loosened, the geckos that ran up and down the whitewashed walls, and spiders and lizards on the stoep. Seagulls blown in from the ocean mewed overhead. A long-neglected windmill creaked in unchecked rusty motion.

He had with him a pocket radio and an iPod for company, a cell phone (for which there was no reception here), a rucksack with shirt, shorts, old sweater, and a broad sunhat. He had some beer and two bottles of Old Brown sherry to go with his coffee in the evenings. And he had the tools of his trade – the GPS unit, compass, survey maps, a geological handbook, twine and pegs, measuring equipment, and of course the shovel and trowel and brushes; and a sieve and pan for sifting. His bakkie bore this load, now parked behind the house. His task was to make an archaeological and heritage impact assessment. The land was to be developed, and law – the national law of heritage – required this.

There was litter in the drift-sand around the house, and like a midden the layers told their stories. First there was the blackened mess against the house wall where vagrants had lit fires; and the charred bits of wood and old ash from these; and all over, the smashed bottles of sweet wine and the condom wrappers and old Coke bottles.

Then, below, came shards of window glass, and then broken pots and plates, but also things that the archaeologist felt he ought to put aside.

He stashed these in a cardboard box – he found a pattern that was mildly interesting: wooden cotton reels; nylon fishing line; rotted hanks of what seemed to be unspun sheep's wool; fish hooks; a cluster of stuff that stank, fish bones and dried fish carcasses. And then some decayed bits of carefully turned and fitted wood – these he placed aside as they emerged from the drifted sand. He saw something in them that he recognised: a spinning wheel, that's what they made up. And more

– framework, hinges, hooks. It struck him then: a spinning wheel, and the remains of a weaving loom. Detritus of the household, the fisherman and his good wife.

And of course the rusty flattened tins. Pathos, it hit him as it always did, the pathos of the more recent past. How long ago? Maybe ten years, fifteen, twenty at most. There were the remains of a small transistor radio in the sand, and it seemed to him that the design was very dated. 1960s. More like forty years then; not of great interest, someone else could pursue it, not him. And pathos was for poets. He didn't have time to waste.

He worked all day on his commission – doing shovel tests for pre-modern middens in the dunes above the tide line, walking the property for features, burial sites, ruins, traces of sheep tracks that might lead to old kraals. He measured, photographed, noted, took cadastral bearings. One more full day's work, he estimated. He didn't expect much. The house itself wasn't worth a detailed heritage assessment. It was surely over sixty years old, requiring a demolition permit; but it wouldn't date long before that and it had no outstanding features, either in its fittings (such as remained) or fabric. If it relayed some social history, that would be different – but there seemed no story attached to this lone dwelling.

He went in to make supper. There was a steel-framed divan with rusty springs beneath the window in the room where he put his camp bed. He settled down, the radio on, a novel to read by the light of a gas lamp. The radio told him news, and he smiled and got up again – he'd forgotten – tonight was a total lunar eclipse, the sun and moon and earth in perfect alignment, and the moon full. He took a glass of sherry and went out on the stoep to look.

The roar of the sea over the sand dunes was accentuated in the dark; also by the pull of the tide, heightened by the rare alignment and the equinoctial swell. The air was full of the saltiness of ocean and he felt invigorated. He gazed up as the eclipse began. The blood-tide running crimson on the moon's old parchment face. The bloody moon above a wine-dark sea. He drank the sherry and dwelt on the associations.

When he first chose archaeology, his mind was on the romance of ancient Greece and Rome, and digging to find Troy, and Ithaca, and such old scenes. He read classics for a year or two, the quaint myths and old epics, the goat-gods, and Orpheus and the underworld, and old Odysseus who sailed the wine-dark seas, as Homer told.

A bloody moon meant signs and wonders for those people. He wondered what it might mean now. Moon and blood and the woman – perhaps this was a time for the female gods. Athena was Odysseus' guide. Did Africa have female gods? Priestesses? He didn't know. He wished he had a companion with him – nice moment for romance but he wasn't good at it. His method was to meet and cut and run, still a bachelor at thirty, growing comfortable in the shabby jeans and sweaters of the field, snug in the reasoning of bone, shell, and ochre. The thought of one called Clementina came into his mind with some remorse. He could have settled with her. Was she watching the eclipse now too?

Time passed. The cold felt damp in his clothes. He left the stoep and went to bed, the blooded moon still in view through the window, its soft red light casting a velvet sheen within the room. Grumbling at his narrow bed, he drifted off to sleep.

He woke to icy damp cold and the keen smell of the sea. *What is going on?* Was the window open? He'd thought it was rusted shut. He raised himself. *What is the time?*

He looked around, and his hair rose on his head, on his arms. His blood ran paler than the pallor of the moon. The divan – on the divan before the window, a form that raised itself like him, on an elbow, a moving form, all wreath of mist and dark light, a tangle of mist. It raised itself on an elbow and turned its head and looked across at him. The sea smell gathered in the room like the deepest depths of ocean, where there's no distinction between the living and the dead.

He froze. He couldn't move, couldn't get up and run. And the door was in the corner near the divan. The smoky-misty head slowly turned and turned, with something like a pair of eyes, and fixed on him. The thing was getting off the divan. It seemed to want a closer look at him . . . There was the silence of a perpetual screaming in his ears, which was his own mind (or his throat, he couldn't tell). And a roaring and a whimpering, which was in him too. And lights in the darkness like the lights of bathypelagic fish that bobbed and glowed and sparkled in his vision. All went red and he passed out.

The cold bright morning found him haggard. It couldn't have happened, he reasoned to himself; but he quickly made his coffee and toast and left the house. Outside it was fresh and less lonesome, with the familiar friendliness of the empty scene. He tramped off with his equipment to focus on the job. Science asked exactitude, which was safe. He measured, noted, dug and measured once again. Only when a seagull cried above him did he start, or when it struck him that he might encounter human remains. The day passed. There was much to do still and he would have to spend another night. He would sleep in the bakkie. He dug on, thrusting all his frame into the work.

The stranger found him crouched with shovel and trowel in his test-pit among the reeds. The stranger was a tall lean man. He had piercing eyes that looked with a distanced curiosity at the sight. He wore tough serge fishermen's breeches and a battered brown corduroy jacket and on his shoulder was slung a canvas bag. In one hand he held a knobkierie, in the other a hessian sack. A knife hung from his belt. On his head, oddly, a green trilby with a feather.

The stranger raised his hand, the heavy stick held high. The archaeologist ducked and flinched, waiting for the blow.

'Hau! *Molo, mlungu!* Do not fear me!'

'Huh?' Still flinching, he raised his head. The tall stranger looked down at him impassively, from his extra height above the digging. The evening sun formed a bright aureole behind this man.

'Ah! I'm – er – *Molo, ndoda*.'

What did this guy want? The raised hand was a salutation, but the man with the spade felt deeply at a disadvantage in the hole he'd dug. He took a long breath, sighed, and scrambled up. 'What can I do for you?'

'Hola! You can make me tea on your stove, please.'

He leant on the spade and stared a bit, then capitulated. 'Come along then. Sit on the stoep. I'll boil the kettle.'

The stranger moved things to make himself a space and sat on the only chair, a splintered bentwood with a broken seat, while tea was made. He took out his pipe, filled it slowly, and when the pot came in applied a match.

Tea was given. Silence. His host, squatting on the stoep wall, felt torn. He wasn't keen to go back inside the darkening house again – but this fellow made things a bit more companionable. The silent presence was alarming; it was also reassuring. The pipe smoke was rich and cherry-fragrant. It led to him going in again and bringing out the open bottle of Old Brown. Sunset, after all. Sherry in tin mugs. A wordless toast from man to man.

The sun slanted quickly down and out, and cold dusk gathered. A bitter thought overwhelmed the archaeologist: he'll move on, and I'll have to face another night here – I can't pack up now in the dark and go – I've got to see it through.

'You have fear, *mlungu*.'

'Eh? What d'you mean?'

'You have great fear. I will tell you why. I know why. I fear too.'

'What do you know?'

'I know – but first, if you please, you tell me what.'

His host shrugged. He got his torch and went back inside, to the dark kitchen at the rear, and returned quickly with bread and jam and the sherry bottle. 'Ja. I'll tell you. But you must understand, I'm a scientist. An archaeologist, you know that? We look for history in the ground, it's lying there in layers – that's why you found me digging that hole.'

'Yes, I understand.'

'So – why must I now have to handle stuff like . . . like . . . All right, last night I discovered that this house is haunted. Crazy, man!'

'What happened, *mhlobo wam?*'

So he spoke of the thing on the old divan, the quality of the dark and the air that moment, the sounds, the surging and the dark light or light dark, who can say? He told this all as best he could, and as he spoke it seemed both nonsense, distant and unreal, and also vivid memory, there again before his eyes. He took a slug of sherry.

'Layers. Yes, I understand. The history in the layers.'

The archaeologist blinked. 'Layers? But that's talking science now. What about this ghostie?'

'What is science? You mean knowledge – *ulwazi?* I will speak.' The stranger blew through his pipe, refilled it, relit, and spoke. 'My name is Malibongwe Ngingingini. I am *isangoma*, you say traditional healer. I too have my science – my knowledge – and this is like yours. It's about the past, which as you truly say is to be found in layers. And sometimes these layers get mixed. *Ingewikkeld, nê? Onderstebo.*'

The thought popped into his host's mind of layered chocolate, milky and bitter. There was a slab inside, in his rucksack. He didn't feel like getting it.

'Go on. Get the chocolate, *mhlobo*. It is safe.'

He stared at the man. 'Serious?'

'Serious.' And the man burst into laughter. 'You call it mind-reading. It's just another level, my friend. All right, I'll fix it, *amafufunyana*, the spell that's on this place.'

The man Malibongwe took dried herbs and a flask from his

bag. 'This is *impepho*, my friend. I will burn it in the house to cleanse it. Come.'

They entered the dark house. Uneasily, the archaeologist showed him the room with the divan. The pit of his stomach recoiled as he went in. It was silent and seemed empty, with no smell now. But the moon, its silver light restored, was bright through the window. His hair rose again.

The sangoma squatted in the centre of the room and made a pile of the dried herbs on an enamel dish. He turned from his host and muttered to himself in isiXhosa.

He spoke louder, and slammed the floor with his hand. He stood upright and shouted, and he leant down and set light to the *impepho*. The smoke dispersed through the room, bittersweet burning herbs. Malibongwe shouted again, spittle flying with perspiration. He took the flask and scattered drops of water in the four corners of the room. He went out in a stamping stagger, the smoke coiling after his inclined tall figure, and he flung the drops of water in the passageway and in each of the other rooms.

The archaeologist made for the stoep; his heart raced and his mind was a mess of unknowing. The shouts continued from inside. Good God, what now? He was trembling. He wished the night was over. It was cold out here – time surely to go and doss down in the bakkie. *What does that crazed witchdoctor propose to do next?*

He froze again: a pale figure sat on the single chair where Malibongwe had been sitting. It sat and looked out at the black ocean with the silver moon. It sat before a loom, and as it gazed it worked the shuttle with an automatic rhythm. It was a woman in her last youth, with long hair and sad eyes, and she flicked and pushed at the shuttle, and it seemed a smile was on her lips, and her eyes were sad but peaceful. And as he stood and stared, the shuttle flew and the silver moon grew brighter and the silver figure faded. And as the shouting in the house died down, she softly disappeared.

He found his face wet with tears. He blew his nose. Malibongwe came outside, exhausted.

'My friend, let me sit down. The *nkosikaz'* has gone now. She'll be all right. She got tangled up for a while. But tomorrow I'm going to need your help with someone else.'

He straddled the bentwood chair. '*Nkos'*. Now where's that chocolate? And I know you've got another bottle of Old Brown. You won't keep secrets from Malibongwe. Where's my pipe? So – a long night ahead, my friend – you and I are going to talk. *Indaba*. Like your *imbongi* Homer and his heroes who held *izindaba* on the islands in the wine-dark sea . . . And pray you, my new friend, who is Clementina?' Malibongwe Ngingingini chuckled deep and soft.

SLATE GREY

Bang! Bang! Bang! WENT THE FIRST OF THE PEBBLES on the grey tin roof. *Bang!* Then a horrid rattling as if huge hailstones were falling. Anna crouched under the formica kitchen table, on the cracked linoleum. She trembled like a reed. She might have wept if she weren't so frightened. She was so thin she could as well have been a reed. Her thin shift was worn, and she was barefoot. She trembled all the more because the vegetables weren't chopped, the meat not prepared, and Tannie Patat due back home at any moment. How would she explain? And what is going on? This banging on the roof, the hail of stones? She could see them bouncing off the cement driveway. The sky was blue. Not a cloud in sight. This wasn't hail. This was something else.

A tin-roofed square old house with a wide stoep filled with junk – broken chairs, an empty aviary, a torn mattress, newspapers and paraffin cans. The windows of the house were like empty sockets. No curtains save for something that sagged in one indecent casement. Some panes were filled with cardboard. The front door was broken. Outside was a bed of dusty cannas, washing on a sagging line. A lone thin dog lay at the end of a chain, barely in reach of his water bowl. People passing by would have avoided the house if it weren't already so set back from the highway and concealed by the mass of flowering mimosa and the keurboom trees.

Anna Persens was sixteen and too slight for her age. Life had stunted her. She was, you could say, a household slave. Brought from a place in the Outeniqua Pass to live with Tannie Patat and Oom Skorsie on a bare plot near Knysna and the tourists, Anna didn't know her parents. She had lost those memories. She had no company of her own age, and no education. But for her first ten years, now long buried, she might have grown up feral.

And perhaps she was. Perhaps she was little more than a wild child of nature who slept and woke and worked, and went through the sullen duties of her day, and fought and bit sometimes, was whipped and wept wild tears and lapsed back into compliance.

Except that something wasn't what it ought to be. How could stones come falling out the sky? Not for the first time either. And now here was Tannie Patat – fat Tannie Patat with her simple face, her nylon dress stretched over her broad stomach and her bandy legs. Under the dress she wore pyjama trousers; her feet in chunky running shoes.

'Anna! Where you? You got vegetables ready?'

Anna crouched under the table.

'Anna? Yoo-hoo!'

She heard Tannie Patat go to the toilet. She peered out of the window. The stones no longer bounced off the driveway. The banging and rattling was over. And her work wasn't done. She shivered, and she got the knife and began her work on potatoes and squashes and carrots.

'What is this? Why you only starting now? You useless one! You lazy!'

Tannie Patat swung out at Anna with her fat fist, but Anna ducked her blows easily. Tannie Patat lost her balance, and her breath. Anna laughed at her, with laughter as her weapon. Raising the stakes, dashing out of the way as Tannie Patat charged. The table took the impact and ground across the floor. The vegetables shot off onto the linoleum. Anna tried to pick them up and Tannie Patat threw her thick body at the girl. Crash they went, against the kitchen sink. Anna slipped out of the breathless woman's clutch and ran outside. The chained dog looked up with little interest. Tannie Patat's wild shouting wouldn't rouse it. Anna went and stood, shivering, in a patch of autumn sun behind the house in the faint fumes of the septic tank.

There were pebbles scattered all around where she stood. Stones that fell from the sky and bounced off the tin roof. She walked away a little. The autumn sun was low. The thick rough pasturage was uneven and in the long grass lay rubbish.

She looked back. The square house with its worn greying paint was sharply lit by the low late sun. It stood against the backdrop of the keurboom trees, and beyond them forests rising up, and above them the strong blue mountain. Before her, the house with dark windows piercing its walls was like a scuffed cardboard model. It fell into strange proportion to her eyes. The fight (as it always did) unlocked something in her mind. She saw, for a short while, clearly. The square grey house seemed to step forward towards her, and into clear focus, and it gathered all its self, its meanness, its dark, its beatings and its drinking into one tight bundle. It was distinct from the stand of trees behind, distinct from the forest and the mountain. So distinct as to be absurd, a kind of vehicle, a conveyance, a container, that had simply come to halt for now.

Anna stepped back further, facing this thing; and she bent forward and reached to it as if pulling it, and – lo! – it lurched a little. She staggered under the movement. She tried again. She stretched her arms out to the house and now she pushed, and the whole thing shuddered and plunged back. She grinned. She tried it again – *faster – pull, push, pull, push.* Working from her thin shoulders, the autumn sun behind her. The house jiggled as if at the end of a long handle. She twisted and it seemed to squeeze towards the side. This way, that way, she twisted and the house squeezed and squirmed at the end of her invisible rod of torque.

She laughed. And then she'd had enough, and clapped her hands and turned her back on the house and wandered on to where the reed beds began, at the edge of the lagoon. The sun's low face glanced strongly off the water. Frogs croaked in the reeds. She listened to them and to the voices of the other creatures of the water. Wouldn't it be nice to be down there, singing with them? The water seemed to call to her. She found a straggle of brambles and ate their late woody berries. Her hem was muddy. The sun! She stood before it, she raised her arms, and to the setting sun she sang.

'*Alweer dronk!*' yelled Oom Skorsie when he came busting in and found Tannie Patat passed out on the kitchen floor. 'You drunk again? And look at what is all the food now – on the floor. No bloody supper and Carlo's here and . . . and this is how we show respect! Where Anna? *Anna!* The bleeding girl!'

And Oom Skorsie settled down to entertain his guest off cane spirit and Coke.

His guest was a dark-haired man with glittering and clever eyes who took the easy chair in the dingy lounge. Carlo. Enterprising Carlo.

'Ja, Skorsie. Cheers.' Carlo gave stout Skorsie a wolf-like grin and settled deeper, looking round and smiling to himself. 'Where your TV, Skorsie?' But Carlo knew the answer – the TV set had broken down and he'd bought it for scrap.

'Hey, Skorsie? What about it then?'

'About what, man?'

'No, just thinking.'

'I'll sort out your cash at the end of the month, Carlo man. You're a good ou. Have some more.'

'Ja, Skorsie. End of the month.' Carlo grinned. 'It's not lekker when you're broke, hey? And all this money like water everywhere.'

'Huh?'

'No, like I mean, here you sit – you and me – in the Garden Route, I say, the Garden Route, tight full of tourists. Loaded with the stuff. Spending like water. Like a drain, Skorsie, like a drain! And you sit here with me like this. Tell me, what's happening with your *meisie* Anna?'

'Ja, Carlo. So it goes, man. Anna. Where Anna? Bloody Patat still passed out in the kitchen. Hey! Anna!'

'Don't call her now, Skorsie. Got an idea for you. Tell me, what does your girl Anna do? Housework, hey? Do you pay her? She does it for free, hey? Board and lodging, am I right? I give you another question: does she pay? What's she now? Seventeen, eighteen? She living for free off you at that age?'

'She just bloody nuisance.'

'Living off of you for nothing?'

'You could say that, ja.'

'Skorsie, how much you got on my slate, hey? You know what, you got nearly five hundred rand on the slate.' Carlo ran the bottle store as well as other things. 'Nice to offer me my own cane, hey, Skorsie?' Carlos grinned broader than ever.

'Ag man, Carlo.'

'No, I mean it, my brother. You need to make more money, man. Milk those fancy tourists. Are you reading me? Know what I mean?'

At the water's edge Anna stood looking at the sun, and she sang a song she learnt from the radio: 'Up-town-girl, da-da di-di dum-dum, up-town-girl.'

And a dark form appeared before the sun, outlined in gold by the rays – a figure from the sun on a boat that came towards her silently, standing and poling the boat towards her, towards the sedge-lined shore. She stood and waited.

The skiff shot up into the reeds. The tall man with the pole steadied himself. He spoke from his dark halo.

'Come, Anna. Get in. No. First go and get the dog – quickly.'

Anna nodded. She ran lightly back to the house, across the thick uneven turf. She went round to the front and grappled with the dog's chain; there was rust of course. Always rust, always. The dog stood up quietly and licked her hand. How to release it? *Oh, quickly, quickly.*

A shout from indoors:

'Anna! You no-good! What for you fiddle with that *brak*? Get inside now. I gon' *donner* you!'

Looming at the window was Patat's simple bulk, and the unclean bulk of Skorsie. And behind them Carlo with the glittering eyes. And they're coming out to get her and the chain won't come free.

Anna worked on the tangled chain. The trio bundled out from the stoep and made for her. Then the dog's mouldy leather collar came right off and he was free. She laughed with relief, and she half carried and half dragged him. But the others weren't encumbered.

'Got you, you little wretch! Carlos! Take her! Quick!'

The dog snarled and bared its teeth.

'Bliksem! The *brak*! Kick it in the teeth, Skorsie!'

'The devil! It's bitten me! I'm bleeding!'

The mêlée punched and kicked and pulled its way back to the stoep. Anna yelled, the dog barked and bit; the others cursed and shoved.

'Hey hey, a right little tiger, isn't she,' puffed Carlo. 'We'll see to that! Got any Dettol?'

They were jammed in the doorway, girl and dog and men. And then it started once again: *rat-a-tat bang*! The pebbles on the roof.

'Who? What that?'

And then more: Anna's pots and pans joined in. She liked to watch them hop around and rattle when she was alone. Sometimes they made up a steel band and entertained her with Jamaican sounds. The spoons tinkled out a nickel harmony while the tin plates gave the beat. The blackened kettle and burnt pots held the bass. They made her laugh when she was on her own. Now they came down like a break-out from a jumble sale. They jangled through the air and they fell upon her foes with clashing din.

'Ah! Ah! Mercy!' cried fat Patat.

'What the donner?' yelled Skorsie, ducking from a steel oven pan.

'Hey! You guys *mal* or what?' Carlos fled, chased by knives and forks.

Anna and the dog seized the moment. They dashed round the house – a final glimpse, and Patat and Skorsie were beating off the ancient pressure cooker as it thundered on their heads. The pan whacked Patat when, hopping, hobbling, she stooped to take a pebble from her shoe.

'Quick, get in,' said the boatman, and he poled the skiff back from the sedge. Up the silvery-tawny path of the setting sun upon the water went the little crew, the tall man at the stern punting carefully, the thin girl and the dog sitting side by side in front. Silhouetted by the sun, they turned their backs to the greying land behind and faced the beauty of the saffron dusk.

MORGENROOD

Anna and the dog were hustled into the back of the archaeologist's bakkie. Malibongwe got into the front beside him.

'Drive, Toby! *Hambani nina!* Go, go, go!' He stared back into the darkness that now clothed the far side of the lagoon.

They drove through the town of Knysna past the stinkwood curio stores and the oyster bars. The pseudo Cape Cod houses loomed with crazy rocking rooflines. Trucks laden with great timber trunks rolled past. In the bistro-glitter of the dusk, tourists milled about avoiding the open hands of the sad descendants of the woodcutters who had made the town. Carlo's Discount Liquors stayed open late for these others who didn't play golf or drink café latte.

Like many of the older generation, Toby's parents had spent their honeymoon in Knysna when it was still a place of romance and solitary peace. Now it was tat and imitation of the same, plus the growing industry of golfing villages. Toby, driving through, had already passed the private polo grounds, the profiles of new money.

The little pick-up hummed through the dark between high woods and forests and the sea that churned below the cliffs. A soft rain fell and in the cab they smelt the khakibos. Toby breathed deep, savouring the fragrance.

'Who's she, then?' he nodded his head to the rear.

'Anna? Thanks for helping, my friend. I'll explain.'

But the sangoma kept his silence for an hour, hugging his knees, while they buzzed westward towards the inky black headlands of Mossel Bay, the old sailors' haven where Vasco da Gama and Bartholomeu Dias and many others over centuries found refuge, water, wood and food.

There the men bundled out for petrol and coffee and hamburgers. Toby opened the canopy door at the back.

'Up-town-girl, da da di di dum,' came a soft sleepy voice, and the dog leapt out and watered the wheel.

'Anna? *Uyaphila*? Are you all right?' Malibongwe helped her out.

'Ooh. I'm stiff.'

They sat down in the chain restaurant.

'*Kahle*, *kahle*,' the sangoma warned. 'The food is fast but please chew slowly for your stomachs' sakes.'

They journeyed on. Little was said. All three had on them the stupor of the long road at night, and Toby's main concern was to stay awake at the wheel.

'One question, please.' Toby broke the silence. 'Why – the other night – when I met you – why did you say you were *cleansing* the house? Was it – the thing – was it dirty, was it vile?'

'No, it's just the word we use. She wasn't unclean. She was trapped in her sadness. I freed her. I did cleanse the house too, in actual fact. I cleansed it of her sadness, so it won't leave traces any more.'

Actual fact, thought Toby to himself.

'Yes, fact of the matter, my friend. No archaeologist will find any traces to record there now.'

Toby bit his lip. He was learning. He'd certainly met with a non-material record in that house.

'And now we've freed Anna too,' said the sangoma happily.

'She a friend of yours?'

'She's my new apprentice,' Malibongwe replied. 'She has been called. She's coming with me to Cape Town to start her training.'

The bakkie ran on through the high sheeplands and wheatfields of the Southern Cape. They passed Albertinia where the aloe factories make salves and unguents from aloe vera sap; the sangoma nodded at them with satisfaction. And on, past Heidelberg and Buffeljagsrivier and the old magistracy of Swellendam, and Riviersonderend and Caledon, and so to the pass that wound its way through the heaving mountains of the great escarpment. Cape Town was still an hour distant, beyond the sandy flats that lay beneath the berg.

'My friend,' said Malibongwe to Toby as they reached the brow of the pass, 'turn off over there.'

In the vague early light of dawn Toby saw a modest gateway and a dirt road leading into trees. Malibongwe gestured them into it.

'We're going for breakfast and a rest. You ought to shave, my friend, before we get to town.'

Toby was too weary to argue. He nudged the bakkie down the track, and presently there came in sight a mellow whitewashed house.

Morgenrood was a converted wayside inn. Built in the early eighteenth century to serve the wagoners who laboured over the mountain pass, its walls were a metre thick with whitewashed lime and stone. The roof was thatch, renewed from the *dakriet* growing on the mountain. Huge beams of yellowwood tied the timbers of the roof, and the floors were large red tiles shipped from Batavia in the long-gone days of the East India Company. The present owners had restored the building and made it into a guesthouse. So well had they done it, Toby thought, casting a professional eye, you wouldn't have thought the centuries had passed. Softest mountain streams flowed into the water pipes, while alien wood, the hakea and wattle, fed the busy boiler. Vrouw Van Winkel, the chatelaine of Morgenrood, was up and making coffee. Heer Rijp Van Winkel fired up his tractor to run the electricity generator behind the house.

Anna was fast asleep in the bakkie. Taking their coffee cups,

Toby and Malibongwe stretched their legs on the mountaintop. They stood and gazed down on the wide sea-girt metropole below. The early air was bracing, laden with the pungent smell of fynbos. Little sugarbirds and sunbirds darted in the thickets of protea.

Ikhwezi, the Morning Star, winked at them and slipped from view. Rosy dawn shot from the east along the Limietberge and Hottentots Holland and the Kogelberg. It caught hoary Hoerikwaggo, Table Mountain, in its first broad stroke and fingered the crowns of Devil's Peak and Signal Hill. It flashed golden off the distant windows of the tower blocks in Bellville and Cape Town, like signals of recognition from the waking city. It reached down and sifted the drifting mists that covered the wide reach of the Cape Flats with its reed pools and dunes and birds now rising in ragged flight. It coaxed the tides of False Bay and Table Bay with rippled light. It called to life – *Vuka! Vukani nina nonke!* – the tens of thousands in the shacks of Khayelitsha and Crossroads, shivering by their smoky morning fires. It glittered on the first of thousands more of workers in their cars, the highways braced for the middle-income morning gridlock. Rijp Van Winkel joined the two men and stood and gazed with undiminished admiration. It was their waking, dawning, the eternal Ay.

Heer Rijp Van Winkel was something of a local sensation. He was born in 1674, in a homestead down below the mountain pass. On a mild autumn day in 1694, taking the sheep into the foothills, he had lain and piped his shepherd's flute, a youth of not yet twenty. Descending from the fastness of the berg came Khoekhoen with their bows and a dart of cunning Morpheus that put the swain to sleep. The sheep (they were the Khoekhoen's rightful fat-tailed flock) departed with those folk, and Rijp slept on for three centuries and a day. Fine mornings were consequently of some importance to Rijp, and he renamed the old tavern Morgenrood to celebrate his hour of rising.

And the crystal mountain air gave virtue to the dawn. The gazers on the mighty scene below drew it deep into their lungs, and felt the heady strength of joy.

'From boys to men,' reflected Malibongwe quietly, looking down the kloof. 'Among my people the young men go to the mountain for their rites of passage. And from girls to women. Now I've got *inkosazana*, a girl, to walk a very special path with me.'

Cape Town at last. The long journey ended in the industrial railway suburb of Salt River, rusted onto the edge of town.

'Here we are,' said Malibongwe Ngingingini. Locomotive Close, a short cul-de-sac in nineteenth-century red brick. At the end was a two-storey brick tenement. The ground floor housed a pet food shop, run by Faisal and Abdurahman Parker.

'My *khaya*'s on the first floor. See if you can wake Anna. We go up those stairs outside.'

A treacherous flight of swaying stairs was bolted to the outside wall. Somehow they stumbled up with Anna limp in their arms. 'Up-town-girl, da da di di . . .' The dog nosed eagerly behind them. The rattle of commuter trains passed within metres of the tenement. Pale faces stared from carriage windows and were swept away across a grid of points.

'One gets used to the trains,' Malibongwe said.

He pushed the door open and Toby gazed for the first time at a shaman's consulting room. Too tired to take it all in, he saw a blur of bottles, calabashes and beads, he smelt a thick blend of herbs and oils and strange galenicals. He thought he saw what looked like dragon's wings and wiped his weary eyes.

'Lay her down there,' said the healer. 'Now – tell me more about Clementina. This *inkosazan'* needs a woman's help.'

Toby felt as though he walked in a dream.

'Clementina? Hang on now . . .' Fatigue made him wrangle. 'Look here, I want to go home and sleep. I could sleep for ever.

Oh, and I don't believe that guy on the mountain was kipping for three centuries. You're having me on.'

'Believe it, *umhlobo wam*,' said Malibongwe. 'I was there. I was called to wake the man. It was even I, back in 1994, who had to learn to play the flute and baa like a sheep. It took six months but I did it. He woke on what is now called Freedom Day. So, now to waken Anna from *her* long slumber; and for this I need your help. Come, ring Clementina if you please.'

WALLFLOWER

Anna Persens, apprentice to the sangoma, was advancing well. Her induction into urban South Africa was complex but she learnt fast. She now wrote with joined-up letters. She was quick at maths too. CACE, the College of Adult and Continuing Education, was pleased with her progress. So was Malibongwe, who had the responsibility of her alternative education under the auspices of the Sector Education and Training Authority, which oversaw the training of indigenous-knowledge practitioners.

After two months of mentoring, Antjie Somers and Katjie Piering, the leaders of Clementina's women's group, felt that her grasp of women's and gender studies was strong enough for her to move into Malibongwe's tenement. She was also counselled on anti-retrovirals, which she needed.

Bureaucracy had been slow to sort out Anna's identity book since there was no birth certificate, but after Malibongwe turned a corridor of officials at Home Affairs into frogs and toads there was no more difficulty. She even got a passport. A driver's licence by legal route would be a greater challenge; but that could wait. Her apprenticeship was, in any event, such that she wouldn't ever really need to drive.

It was a privilege to live and work with Malibongwe. She looked around his studio, taking in again the rows of rare creatures on the walls, the manticore and bunyip, wendigo and hobeya. A stuffed dodo and a coelacanth were the pride of his collection, alongside the glass case of little mantises. There were rich skins – of leopard and lion, quagga, aurochs, and giraffe. Books of recipes and of wisdom lined one wall, and there were filing cabinets, cases, drawers, racks for drying herbs, and, in the centre of the room, his consulting couch in zebra skin.

Anna glanced up at the autochrone, the unique longcase clock that young Rijp Van Winkel had given Malibongwe in gratitude some years back. Malibongwe had gone off now on his Yamaha motorcycle to do a house call at the night shelter up the road in Woodstock. The vagrant Ougat Wolf, kaptein of the Hoerikwaggo bergies, was ill, they said; had ditched his supermarket trolley. Before Malibongwe returned, Anna had to fill the water cistern from the well down in the yard (water magnetised with quartz and enriched with minerals from deep below the earth's brown crust) and she wanted to sweep and clean the studio. She also meant to press his exotic purple dashiki shirt and flowing agbada. He was off to a dinner of the temperance league, the Order of True Templars, in the evening and she wanted him to look his best. The fragrant purple and yellow wallflowers she had picked from the yard were wilting. She hummed the words from a Dylan song that Clementina'd taught her:

'Wallflower, wallflower, won't you dance with me?'

The autochrone showed seventy degrees off the conjunction of Crux Australis and the sun. Time for tea. This fine baroque longcase clock had been in Rijp's family since their arrival in the Cape in 1660. Made by masters in the Amsterdam studio of Siderius van den Berg, it was a wonder of horology. Miniature barques rocked on a carved and painted sea, and the little planets in their spheres jiggled and rolled their way across the ornate face while the fretted sun and moon sailed over a firmament patina'd in golden filigree. The clockwork was energised not by winding but by gentle trepidation. The rumbling of the trains on the railway line behind the tenement was adequate for this.

Anna made herself a cup of rooibos and filled Nostril's water bowl. She sighed as she looked into the cistern of mineral water to be sluiced and filled. Some of the tasks he set were *ukuthwala*, challenges that tested fortitude and strength. Success would bring *ukuthwala* unto her – empowerment, as the term now goes. But oh, the deep well outside, the swaying staircase, the heavy bucket, it was a labour to get this done. She picked up the new broom she'd bought from a passing vendor, a simple affair of fragrant brown reeds tied to the end of a stick. She liked it. The reeds gave off a rich old scent that mingled with the peachy wallflowers.

'Oh, won't you dance with me?'

Would she? Could she? She sat down, reflecting on the passage of her long training. Already she could make the kitchen utensils do half her work for her, and play percussion while they did it. Her textbooks turned the pages of their own accord. She could make sash windows go up and down and doors close and open. One thing she knew, and that was not to tamper with the outside world. Once only, and only for a moment, had she been tempted to try her powers on the grid of railway points. Along with her native powers, it was instinct that qualified her for training as a healer – a warm heart and an instinct for all that's good. Of course she was mischievous and unpredictable. She was a good-looking and talented young woman. But she wasn't irresponsible. She never ever tampered with the railway system or with traffic lights.

What happened now was, as Malibongwe later wisely said, to be foreseen. She galvanised the broom and energised the bucket. Had she but known it, she was opening the floodgates of social change in southern Africa. For generations the women of the nation swept and drew water for their men or for those who hired them as servants. From distant pump or leaking rural standpipe, the women of the nation toiled with plastic vessels of all sizes, bearing the precious resource to kraal and village, settlement and town. Provision of accessible clean water was high on the national agenda. For Anna, it made common sense to get her chores done quickly. If her gift was universal, how much easier the burden of the womanhood of Africa! Why, even thirsty men might then consider drawing water for themselves.

But first, now, the broom.

Anna held it upright on the floorboards and smiled encouragingly at it. She let go, and it fell to the floor. She held it up again and scowled. It fell and twitched a little. The third time, she took another swig of rooibos, closed her eyes, and got the pulses going freely in her mind. She felt the broom jiggle in her hand at last. Now! Go to, new broom of chosen reeds, and do your work!

To her delight, the broom took a tentative sweep around her. Then it plucked up courage and moved out across the floor. It trembled with eagerness and began to dance about the room. It kicked up a storm of little dust devils and Anna sneezed. Geckos hastened from its path. Nostril barked and gambolled with the besom as it gathered up his loose hairs. 'Yo,' thought Anna, 'cool!'

Now she turned to the bucket. '*Asseblief?*' She spoke to it politely. Nothing. The vessel looked up at her in plaintive silence. 'Oh, I'll just empty you out first! *Sorry.*' She stooped and took out Malibongwe's mouth organ where she'd hidden it, and his pipe and a litter of spare electric plugs and light bulbs and shoe brushes and dusters and candles and polish tins. 'Now – OK!'

And lo, the modest bucket tipped and swayed and waddled around in circles.

'Yes! Oh yes! Keep going, little bucket! Now – see that cistern?'

Next, Anna opened the door to the outside stairs. 'It's steep, hey? You be careful. Down there – the well, you understand? Hey, hey, hey!'

The bucket took a tumble, clanging step after step all the way down. At the foot, in Malibongwe's yard, it shook itself and ambled to the well. While Anna watched from above, it teetered on the brink, carefully filled itself, and began its laden return. One step, two, up it came; and inside, and (slopping just a little) plodded to the cistern, and emptied itself of its litres. It set off once again.

Meanwhile the broom danced *vastrap* – polkas and quicksteps and foxtrots round and round the studio.

'*Balke toe!*' cried Anna in delight. 'Give it stick!'

It stopped for a beat or so and bowed to her – an invitation to the dance. The spoons began a simple waltz rhythm on the kitchen sink, and Anna went up to the broom and demurely accepted its embrace. Off they went – *one*-two-three, *one*-two-three, round and round and round. The beat quickened to a two-step; and a cha-cha; and then, why, the broom was pushing for a tango! But the spoons began a crazy tarantella, and breathless, out of her depth, Anna had to break off. The castanet clatter from the sink was heady stuff; the broom twirled and leaped and filled the room with scent of reedy wetlands. Dance a cachucha, fandango, bolero! With a glint on its meniscus, the stolid little bucket paused in its damp circuit for a while to watch.

And then the breakdancing began. The broom was showing off. Freestyle. The silver spoons had no taste or talent for rap; they fell silent while the broom tossed itself in the air, slammed on the floor, spun round and round, did headstands. That brown reed broom was masterless. It ran about and flung itself against the walls. It brought streaming cobwebs down on the furniture. It knocked off bits of plaster. Now it seemed to want to sweep the workbench clean! Malibongwe's retort, his pipette and tubes and bottles! His powders kept in open bowls, his piles of scripts. Anna had to stop it now.

She screwed up her courage and grabbed the energetic broom, and, flinching, broke it over her knee. But to her astonishment there were now two brooms (slightly shorter, granted) but a pair. They twisted from her hands, ran to opposite sides of the room, and then, to a cymbal clash from the saucepan lids, they came together in a flying *pas-de-deux*. The mop joined them and they tripped across the floor, sticks linked, like three long-necked swans. Then the mop stood out from the dance and the other two engaged in a passionate tango while it looked on. The mop aimed its handle at them, the steak mallet banged on the boiler, and one dancer fell. The other threw itself about in anguish. Then the players all arose, bowed to Anna, and with tripping movements ran from the floodlights to the wings.

*Flood*lights? Anna noticed to her horror that the cistern was overflowing. In the glamour of the dance she'd forgotten all about the bucket. As she watched, the little glinting pail sloshed in another ten litres, and the water slopped onto the floor. And off it went for more. Dogged, set with steely intent, it plodded out and back again. And the water sluiced from the cistern across the room. The brooms leaped up onto Malibongwe's consulting couch and huddled together. To and fro went the bucket, resisting Anna's strength and her novice charm. Nothing seemed to stay its course. There was something – something (surely not petulance?) in its silent purpose.

Anna ran and placed plastic bowls and tubs to catch the overflow but these too grew full. She poured them out into the lavatory and the bath; she threw the water out of the window; she thought she gained on the plodding bucket, but still it came, and still it poured and filled and waddled to and fro. There seemed no limit to its goal. She looked at the mop with some misgiving but it was behaving now, and she grabbed it and worked at pushing wavelets of water out onto the stairs. The brimming bucket stumbled up the steps and pushed brusquely past her.

'Help! Oh, help! Nostril, fetch your master. Go, go, go!' She flattened herself against the wall, perched on a footstool above the rising waters. Nostril got up beside her.

'Hey there! In the name of names, what's going on?' It was the voices of Faisal and Abdurahman Parker from the pet food shop below: 'Hey you, you up there! You're leaking!'

'Hola,' called out Malibongwe as he took off his motorcycle helmet in the yard below. 'Old Wolfie's gone back to meths again, the blue train. Anna? Are you there? Are you in the bath? Remember I'm out for supper – got a formal dinner.'

'Help! I'm sorry, I didn't mean . . .'

Malibongwe rushed up the dripping stairs. He gazed within and the bucket jumped, spilling a few litres. The brooms ducked behind the cushions on the couch. Anna hid her face in her hands. Malibongwe smiled, and '*Phantsi! Thula, thula! Uxolweni!*' he called sternly. 'Down, down, be peaceful now.'

He strode to the precious autochrone. He reached inside and pulled on cords. The sprockets whirred, the little barques tossed furiously, the planets whizzed around their courses. The room flickered and the water evaporated in a shining mist. Dust settled on the floor. The bucket and the broom took up their modest stations, and Malibongwe crept out quietly, to re-enter upon a peaceful homely scene. Anna sat pondering among her books. Nostril slept at her feet.

'Hola,' called out Malibongwe, taking off his helmet. 'Ougat's been on the meths again. Anna? Time for tea. Must I fill the kettle?'

AFRICAN VIOLET

THE GARDEN, LIKE ALL GOOD GARDENS, WAS LAYERED. It had a variety of prospects, depending on where one stood. A tall hedge of old myrtle hid a herb garden with a stone sundial. A thicket of wild almond closed off a lawn that ran down to a terrace, and then below that a sunken garden fringed with varieties of sage and lavender. To the north-east of the house was a rose garden with old-fashioned English roses, and climbers rambled on a weathered brick wall. To the north was the mountain, now a dark violet in the shadow of lowering cloud. Opposite, the view over the terraces spilt out over a great valley and the sea. Westward was thick with ironwood, assegai, wild olive, cork oak. To the east ran the winding road and the driveway, hung with bougainvillea and wisteria and wild Cape vine.

Lady Camphorwood was nearly eighty but undiminished in spirit. She wore a wide straw hat and a gardening smock and wielded her secateurs like the judge's gavel, the teacher's cane, the geometrician's pair of compasses. Her fond eye took her unerringly from japonica to azalea to hibiscus. Spiky as her stand of aloes she was, lone as the tall Australian flame tree, serene as the cypresses guarding the terrace steps, simple as the tiny sutera and penny royal between the paving, tough as kikuyu, rich within as the best of compost heaps.

She did not believe in fairies at the bottom of the garden though there was a kind of one in the garden shed.

'Call me the Queen of Spades,' jested Cecil Syster, her epicene gardener. 'All I ask for is a row of ranunculus and a big hairy euphorbia. Aren't these tubers divine?'

'No doubt, Cecil,' said Lady Camphorwood austerely, 'but I need a cup of tea. Call Ethelreda, will you? The weather's changing. It looks like a northerly storm, don't you think?'

She stalked towards the terrace, and Cecil ducked into the farthest corner of his shed where he tenderly groomed his crop of cannabis behind the row of African violets he was propagating.

'You and Five Roses, darlings. One lump or two?' He watered the little green rootlings with loving care. '*En wat van 'n lekker happie groenkoek ook? Dit sal die tee nou lekker laat smaak.* Bend your mind with Cecil's bong. Open up to amazing prospects. Grow, my little dingetjies, grow nicely for your Cecil.'

The ravines of Hoerikwaggo hung above the woods behind the house. The north wind poured dark cloud down the sandstone face, through the thick growth of erica, protea and silvertree. Colonel Jim's shadow turned and twisted in the boiling mass of cloud. Cold swept down; rain came in sheets and tossed the tops of gums and pines. Malibongwe crouched beneath a great old oak, his cape around his shoulders. 'Eish! I feel him close. *Hamba*, Black Jim!' He shivered, wishing he was back in his studio. He hoisted his sack of roots and leaves, blister plant and buchu and sluimbal, medicinal herbs gathered by permit up above the tree line. '*Akukho wena namhlanje*, Black Jim!'

Like Adamastor, the old Titan spirit of Table Mountain, like Van der Decken, the flying Dutchman condemned for aye to tack about the stormy Cape, Colonel Jim was bound by karmic law to haunt these woods and mountains. Sometimes he was found in the flying South-easter; sometimes in the black northerly gales; sometimes hovering over the Hottentots Holland and then swooping back along the Langeberg and the Outeniqua and the Tsitsikamma and the Langkloof to the Amatola Mountains of the Eastern Cape, where his blood and the blood of his victims were long fused black into the roots of ferns and aloes and cycads in distant kloofs. The heart and body of Ntshona Koloni and of Mpuma Koloni was haunted by the spirit of Colonel Jim. The old Colony had him bound to its earthy self; a thing that gripped its spine, that crawled its limbs, that posted to and fro along its red veins. Black Jim. Colonel Jim. And Colonel Jim was Malibongwe's old adversary.

Right now there was another kind of adversary. Malibongwe made his way, as the rain and wind beat stronger, down to Camphorwood House for a cup of tea with Cecil Syster and a word with Lady Camphorwood. They were old acquaintances. This time there was bad news – a bulldozer and a team with chainsaws, waiting for the rain to pass.

'Development in Klaasenbosch?'

'Not in the bosch, Malibongwe, in place of it. They want to clear the whole thing. Every tree. Build twenty houses. Tuscan, if you please.'

'The whole forest?'

'The whole forest.'

'Tuscan?'

'Tuscan.'

Not Florence and the valley of the Arno and the hill *villaggi* she knew as a child. Not these but an invention from Gauteng. Lady Camphorwood looked out through the long west window at the mass of trees, their crowns tossed in the rising gale. Something wonderful about the dark boles, the depth of a wood, the promise of living mystery within. She loved Klaasenbosch in every season, every mood. The way the sunlight whitened on the bark, the moss dark on the southern side of the trunks, the light that filtered through the canopy, the earthy acid tang of autumn leaves, the aureole of early green in September.

The thought of it all gone, of twenty Tuscan townhouses, of yards of brick paving and high yellow walls, electric fences, ostentatious cars and security guards and perimeter lights and hedges of tiresome eugenia if they even rose to that degree of greenery. And that would be the end of the colony of orioles, the cisticolas and nightjars, the squirrels (nuisance that they were), the shy porcupine, owls. It would be the end of brooding silence and of sudden small joys.

It would be the end, the end, and yes maybe we've had it all too good for all too long, and who can stay the hand of progress? (She shuddered. 'Progress.' Wrong word.) The developers had the gall to claim they meant to stabilise the land. Stabilise! She snorted. The slant they put on things. And folk swallow it too. Who cares these days? Who cares indeed. She was tired.

Malibongwe spoke. 'There may be no graves, but there is something else.'

'Graves?'

'If there were old graves, if there were an old burying ground, then the owners would be forbidden to build on it. Muslim, Christian, there would be grounds for stopping them.'

His friend the archaeologist Toby Graaff had gone over the details of the National Heritage Resources Act with him: 36.3 (a) was the clause in question, but since Malibongwe had no evidence of graves the point was academic.

'Well . . .'

'But listen. I know for a fact (Malibongwe's facts were legion, not all of them empirical but all with a cogency of their own), I know for a fact a certain clan once lived there – Khoekhoen people – not my people – long ago. I hear them when I'm gathering herbs. Let me think about this.'

No question of restoration of this valuable land to those who had been wiped out in the early eighteenth century through smallpox and through violence. Little chance of taking on the big companies in the courts on grounds of clairvoyancy. Glumly she scried the tea leaves at the bottom of her cup.

Malibongwe rose and wandered through the spacious house. Lady Camphorwood let him go. She stared unseeing through the window.

Sir Ambrose's study stood much as it was in his day, much

as it was in the day of his father the baronet. Whitewashed wall with a casement window; dark wood and leather; a roll-top desk; bookshelves to the ceiling; an ancient Remington typewriter; an oar with college colours and the team inscribed; and, on the wall, framed photographs. There he was, the old baronet, at Buckingham Palace and at Sandringham, one-time equerry to George V; there was his son Sir Ambrose as an undergraduate at Cambridge in his tennis kit; team photographs; regimental photographs. Sir Ambrose in his uniform as lieutenant in the Blues and Royals. And there, on a wooden stand, a brass helmet and plume, a cavalry cloak, the full dress headgear of a heavy dragoon.

Malibongwe stopped in his tracks. 'Hau! Black Jim!' Colonel Jim, colonel of dragoons. The dread colonel seemed for a moment to be in the cramped room. The curtain tossed in the breeze. The door swung to behind Malibongwe. A faint sinister chuckle teased his ear.

He shook his head. No, this figure in the photograph was not the Adversary. This was a porky good-natured sporting boy, pink and eager, soon to wed the honourable Sarah Bligh, now Lady Camphorwood. All this Malibongwe knew or, rather, intuited as he scanned the old trophies. Why then the fear?

Malibongwe stood silent, focusing, listening, reflecting. Then it came to him: Why not? Why not use that dread force? Grasp old Black Jim (for here he is, palpably) and dupe him and use him in this present crisis? A dangerous ploy. He, Malibongwe, would be the stalking horse. A very dangerous game to play; but, given the stakes and dear Lady Camphorwood, a risk worth taking. One thing in common between Lady Camphorwood and her late husband and him, Malibongwe himself, and indeed his feared adversary, Colonel Jim, one thing, and that was the love of land. Love of woods and forests, of pastures and open meadows, animals and the veld. Somehow to marshal the malice of Black Jim, and turn it to good use. Could he pull it off?

'Lady C,' called Malibongwe, 'may I borrow Cecil for an hour?'

'Cecil? My dear Malibongwe, whatever for? How is your friend Anna? You must bring her to tea again one day.'

'Cecil.' Malibongwe bearded him in his shed.

'Oh, Malibongwe.'

'Look, you and me, we've got to help Lady Camphorwood. I've got an idea. Do you mind dressing up?'

Cecil was amused with the brass helmet and its red plume, with the frogged tunic and the riding cloak of the Blues and Royals. He tugged on the thigh boots with their spurs.

'*Lekker goed hierdie!*' All a few sizes too big for slight and wiry Cecil, but the effect would do.

'Stand still, Cecil! Don't make any sudden moves!'

'*Hoesê? Wat is aan die gang?*'

'Sh. Just stand to attention. Upright, man! It's Black Jim. Don't worry, I won't let any harm come to you. He thinks you're one of his men, his troopers.'

'Super trouper, super-duper trouper.' Cecil sashayed in his kit.

'No, Cecil! Don't mess around! Here he comes!'

And sure enough, the wind gathered and darkened and a force came whistling through the garden and thickened and twisted before the little shed. Pots and mulch and empty fertiliser bags were caught up in this black whirlwind.

'O *Jirre!*' cried Cecil. 'I promise I'll never smoke another zol!'

'Whoooooh,' whistled the black twister. 'Whooooh, whoooooaah!'

Malibongwe stepped aside, and the dust devil seemed to bend between him and Cecil. 'Whoooooh! Whooooh are yooooo, yoo horrible little troooooooper? Whooooooh, whoooh, whoooh?'

Malibongwe's instinct was on target. The sight of Cecil in his kit had drawn the quarry. Now to lead it to the task in hand.

Cecil had a potted African violet in his hand; he was about to hurl it at Black Jim. Malibongwe cried out, diverting the Adversary's attention: 'Ya! *iKolonel wa dragoni!* Ya! Fat loser, one whose sword is broken, one who cannot win, big failure of Queen Victoria, bragging old fall-off-his-horse, big loser to the amaXhosa, remember the Amatola! Ya!' Malibongwe ducked behind the shed as he taunted the dark form.

It convulsed and came at him; right through the shed, wood flying in the air, African violets and cannabis among the broken planks.

Malibongwe ran, ducking beneath the fury of the dark wind. He ran down the terraces, towards the woods, into the trees, flying over leaf mould and thick roots. He headed for the lower fringe of trees, just above the road where he saw the truck and chainsaw team, the bulldozer, the agent and surveyor and developer with their map. Casting a quick glance at the demon as it blustered on behind him through the trees, he broke out into the open. The workmen stopped and stared at him. Already saws were buzzing, the vicious mosquito buzz of dendrocide. Then they saw the thing that followed.

'Whooooooo! Whaaaaaa! Whaaa whaa what is going on?' Black Jim thundered and spewed rain and dark wind about him. 'Hoooo hooo horrid! Horrible little men! Yooooo who doo to wooods, yooooo, yooo! Cavalry, Charge!'

Some say they saw that rainy day in the upper woods of the Constantia Valley a ghostly charge of cavalry. Some say these claims are crazy, things seen as a result of what some people get to smoke these days. But there are those who say a squadron of ghost riders came out of Klaasenbosch and rode at them from out of the trees, on horses whose manes tossed in the wind, their cloaks billowing, their plumes flowing from great brass helmets, like something out of the movies, so they say, but like only weird, and there were sabres in the air, and the thunder of hooves, and a force like electricity (maybe the lightning struck them) and then the bulldozer was lifted like a toy, and the lorry too, and thrown into the river gully; and the chainsaws wrenched from their hands (see, sprained wrist to this day), and carried up, up, in a dark whirlwind that gained the mountain's height, then sped out to the blue reach of False Bay where it rained chainsaws briefly into the deep.

That wasn't all. A murmuring and chattering in the woods. Brown bodies in karosses slipping through the trees. Shades of long-dead Khoekoen who had woken to the passing of the squadrons of the air.

Malibongwe turned back between the tree trunks. He stayed there for an hour, on his haunches in the deepest thicket. *Indaba*. He parleyed with these people. 'Take back your own. You can do it. Never let them take your forest. Not the way those *umlungu* did it. Not with rage and violence. Do it softly, do it slowly, do it deeply in quiet ways until your mind is the mind of this place again and even more. Let your mind grow here until it takes charge. Then others will know it too; they will leave this wood alone. I have spoken.'

Indoors Cecil lay on Lady Camphorwood's sofa, a sorry sight in wet and muddy cavalry cloak, his legs in the air.

'Pull, Cecil, pull!'

They got the boots off him and spooned a sherried gazpacho into him with just a touch, a *titseltjie*, of bong.

'Well done, Cecil,' said Malibongwe. 'It was very well done.' How sustainable the defence had been he could not tell. There was going to be more work of this kind – the stakes were high, and the risk was great.

He picked a shy little African violet out of a boot. 'I'll take this to give to Anna, if I may.'

SILVER FISH

'THAT WAS A STORM LAST NIGHT,' John Dory reflected. 'Waves, three-metre waves, clean over the harbour wall.'

'Ja, right up to the railway line,' said Dirk Galjoen. 'And you know what? There we are – running for shelter behind Seal Island. A high swell. Next thing – bang! And a bloody great two-stroke chainsaw falls into the boat! Slap-bang from the clouds. Nearly went right through the bottom.'

'Ha!' replied Red Roman, a wrangling sort of chap. 'Tell that to the guys in Simon's Town.'

'Did I tell you about the mermaid I caught off Bellows Rock?' Stumpnose Jones joined in, winking. 'Man, she was pretty.'

'Did she like you?' asked John Dory.

'Dunno – she got away.'

'Don't be scaly! I'm telling you!' insisted Dirk Galjoen. 'Listen, would I lie? There's still some fuel in the chainsaw too. Want to see?'

'Sure, sure,' said Red Roman. 'You could see my freezer chest and I could say it fell off the back of an aeroplane.'

Pedro Bonito interrupted:

'Talk of freezers! I've got something you won't believe. There isn't flounders in False Bay, is there? I mean . . .'

'Flounders? You doesn't get flounders here, my brother. There isn't no flounders in the Cape. Not that there's much else left any more either, am I right?'

'That's what's so fishy, like I said. I looked it up in a book. For sure it's a flounder; except it's bigger than they say. It's massive. Takes up the whole freezer. Wife's excited. She wants to make it into steaks.'

Red Roman, John Dory, Dirk and Pedro trooped into Pedro's cramped cottage.

'Oh yeah? Flounder, hey? Massive flounder, like what you saw in a book? What you been reading then? What you smoke? Does your flounder speak? Give it a shout and ask it where it's hiding.'

'But – but – I swear. On my grave. *Juanita!* What you done with my flounder?'

'Yeah, yeah. Flounder's gone down to the Brass Bell for a pint, my friend. Let's go and join it. Perhaps it's got a wallet too. There's a luck.'

But handsome Juanita is already going out with the flounder. 'Mother Mary, Star of the Sea, and all the Saints be thanked and praised,' she patters out her orisons. 'For this flounder thanks I give.'

She carries it over her shoulder and it trails almost to the ground. She pants. She perspires a little, not just from the burden but from anxiety. The silvery-scaled great flounder is draped in a large raincoat on her shoulder. Pedro mustn't know – it'll be a surprise for him. She staggers a bit as she crosses the road. Down to the harbour where she can clean and scale it on the fish market's concrete slabs. There's no one else about at this late hour. She has a torch in her pocket and a large sharp knife.

She reaches her goal and slings the great fish off her shoulder.

'*Ouch!*' says the fish.

'Ey?' asks Juanita.

'Ouch, I said. Be a bit more gentle on a fish, good mother.'

Kalk Bay on the coastal railway line to the naval base of Simon's Town is an old-established fishing village. It has a harbour for the boats, a fish market, and tenements and poky terraced semis, where the fishermen and their families live. The mountain climbs steeply up behind, and in front is the shining sea. The streets ramble up the mountain's lower slopes, making a picturesque jumble of tin roofs. So picturesque it is that many fishermen no longer can afford their little cottages. For some time Kalk Bay has been home to bohemians of all sorts who find authenticity in the working village. There are painters and poets, craftsmen and antique dealers, outlets for collectables and bright New Age clothes and crystals. Corner shops where red bait and fishing hooks and sinkers might be bought are now coffee shops and boutiques of common and rare bijouterie.

Bohemians themselves are subject to the laws of change. Where once the boutiques vended incense and bronze buddhas and books by Sri Sri Swami Vedanta, now they cater for retired university lecturers from Johannesburg and sell revisionist histories and refills for Waterman pens, and African masks in jacaranda wood.

Juanita finds it difficult these days to buy a rosary in Kalk Bay, just as her man Pedro has to go further afield for a hook and line and sinker. Hard times have hit the founding Filipino fisherfolk, with crazy quotas imposed on them and less fish to go around, and fewer lodgings that they can afford to rent. Some of them are friends of the sangoma Malibongwe Ngingingini, and his apprentice Anna Persens.

'Santa Maria!' cries Juanita Bonito. 'A talking fish! Ah, *maravilha! Milagre!* A miracle!'

'If you say so,' says the flounder wetly.

'O Santa Lucia! I must go and tell Father João at once!'

'And leave me here on this cold slab? In the dark? Oh no you don't.'

'I go! I go now! I fly! Father João! Father João!'

'Woman! What's it worth to you to go running off right now?'

'I go! Oh praise be, a miracle! Oh, fame, oh fortune rains her blessings on us, fame and fortune, *maravilha!* Wonder! Joy!'

'I can do you better,' sighs the flounder. 'Much better. Hold your horses. Let me speak.'

'Ey?'

'Just give me a word or two edgeways,' says the flounder looking up with watery eye. 'This isn't small fry, get me? You cut me into steaks, you lose. You take me to your priest, you also lose. He'll keep me and eat me for himself – I know all about the Friday thing.'

'So why we go hungry and have no miracles?'

'I'll explain.'

Handsome Juanita lights a cigarette and sits on a bollard while the flounder marshals its thoughts.

'Woman. True enough to say you've been taken by surprise. Small wonder. Look, just pour a bucket over me, will you? A fish can get dehydrated out here.'

Juanita obliges.

'Thank you, good wife. Do my silver scales lie smooth? I wish you'd give me a quick rub down while I'm damp. Ah. Thank you. I will proceed.

'From northern seas I steered my way. By star by night and sun by day I navigated through the gates of golden Hesperus.'

'Ey?'

But the flounder's eyes are glazed, his jaws uplifted to the starry sky, and on quoth he. 'Atlantis and its moss-girt towers, its denizens and their deep demesnes, lay 'neath my shining course. Caravels and galliots all wrought with gilt and laden by their bootless cannon swayed above the sandy bed, in aye perpetual conveyance of drowned souls.'

'Ooh.' Juanita shivers.

'Of drowned souls. Past Biscay's driven sands and Tagus' oozy flood I gained the bulk of Lusitania. How am I doing? What comes next?'

Juanita shrugs.

'Wait . . . Yes. Then Afric's golden shore espied, I found the Moor and Bedou by and by in simple dhow and white felucca borne up on the water's breast. Corsair of Barb'ry and the booming carronade made lattice of their sail but I, inured of harm, among the soft-eyed halibut did glide and swim. The seas were sunny and of bluest glaze and southern sirens sang their charms to me. Sang their charms I say, and swept the harp of seaweed true. Anyway, to cut a long story short, I pushed on past the kings of Timbuctoo and Dahomey, and what they call Angola. And then Namibia, Walvis Bay (ugh) and the tedious Northern Cape with all those blinking seals, and I got here last night and a bloody great wave washed me, what do you know, right out of the freaking sea and onto the railway line. And if it wasn't for your bloke just hopping over the tracks from the pub for a short cut home, I would've caught it right and proper from the last train out of Simon's Town. And then I spends a night in your ruddy freezer and here we are and ain't it nice and cosy on this slab, don't I think?'

'Santa Maria! You come a long way then!'

'Ay. It be a long and wat'ry path I beat upon the ocean's back. Anyway, here's the deal. I've got to grant you three wishes. I grant you these, you wish 'em, I go back in t'ocean, you get your wishes. You happy, me happy. See?'

'See.'

'Fine. Come on then.'

'What I do?'

The flounder sighs. 'Must I spell out everything? Just like you've passed your catechism – am I right? You got to say the words like they're meant to be said. In the proper order and so forth.'

'I don't know the words.'

'Very well. Repeat after me: "Flounder, flounder, from the sea—"'

'"Flounder, flounder, from the sea—"'

'"What is it you've got for me?"'

'"What is it you've got for me?"'

'Knock knock.'

'Who's there?'

'Flounder.'

'Flounder who?'

'Flounder who astound 'er. Wa ha ha!'

'Sies, man, be lekker.'

'Sorry. All right. We cut to the chase. Make a wish, good woman.'

BANG! The barroom of the Brass Bell, the railway tavern that stood poised above the rocks and tidal pool, seemed to change its shape. The bottle racks and glasses swayed.

'Oof!' said Pedro Bonito. 'Either that was a goods train passing or I've had one too many.'

'Agh, forget it, man, it's nothing.' Red Roman, John Dory, Dirk Galjoen and Pedro Bonito knocked back their pints and ordered a final round. The Linefishermen's Glee Club had been installed in the pub for a long, long session.

'Ja well . . . no flounder here, Pedro. Did it get away then? Ha ha ha!'

'Sh, man, quiet, it's Joe Maasbanker's turn.'

Joe Maasbanker was a solo artiste who did original jazzy numbers. 'I'm the snoek from Kalk Bay,' he sang, 'I'm the one that got away. At night, while you sleep, into your bed will I creep; I'm the snoek, I'm the snoek, I'm the snoek from Kalk Bay.'

'He may be talented but he's a real skate, that one.'

The packed bar rose and joined as one man in the closing favourite, 'Santa Lucia'. To its strains they paid their tabs and rolled shouting, singing out onto the railway platform. Swinging themselves down onto the tracks (fishermen don't use subways), they streamed back to the Main Road and their own steep silent streets and waiting wives.

Santa Lucia, Santa Lucia!
Sul mare luccica, l'astro d'argento,
Placid' è l'onda, prosper' il vento,
Venit' all' agile barchetta mia,
Santa Lucia, Santa Lucia.

The words meant little, but the throbbing gist and falling cadence were clear to hearts made glad with wine and fellowship and song. A glad sadness that called up old sorrows unknown though crystal clear, and sheer joy of shining sea and stars and moon, the weeping heart and flush friends and a barmaid of such beauty-o, the pain, the joy, the years that pass with time and tide. John Dory tripped and fell on the tracks and was hauled up onto the northbound platform by Red Roman and Dirk Galjoen and Pedro Bonito. They wept and laughed and were led by instinct to the humble home of Pedro.

'Oh, my Juanita, how she loves me so!'

'You sure? It's almost three.'

'Of course, of course. Come in, she'll make us coffee. No problemo, my friends. No problemo.'

And with expansive gesture, Pedro swayed and fell flat up a side alley.

'Steady as she goes.'

'Don't rock the boat.'

'Heave ho and up she rises.'

They got him home, and found his key, and aimed for a while at the keyhole.

'Pedro? Hey, Pedro! There *is* a problem. Your key don't fit this hole.'

And Pedro raised his weary visage and gazed upon his humble home.

'Nay! *Nooit*! What this? Where you taken us?'

'Home, old salt.'

'But – just check . . .'

And check they did: No. 2, Adam's Alley. Sure as wine

and malt aren't spirits, it was the right address. But what was wrong?

For fifteen years Pedro and Juanita Bonito had lived and loved and worked and kept the faith in No. 2, Adam's Alley, Kalk Bay – a two-bedroomed tin-roofed semi with thick crumbling walls and rotting windows, no hot water, and outside loo, but home it was and home it meant. Go inside and see the fact. There's the lounge suite, there's the barrel of salted snoek, the TV, the walls of shiny pink and green enamel paint, the sink frilly with fish scales, the poster of the Bleeding Heart. At least the place was rent-controlled and occupation guaranteed.

But what was this? The property value of No. 2 had shot up some several hundreds of per cent. What stood before them in the street was a shining mass of Tuscany and Acropole all blended into one. The façade bore a pediment and pedestal and portico of white marble. Elegant Ionic columns held up the moneyed grace. Behind were row upon row of high windows, faintly tinted, that showed the rooms within. These, lighted with great chandeliers, were empty (in the modern mode) save for a great grand piano and some reeds in silver bowls. While the fishermen gaped, a door swung open and lo, Juanita made her passage down the generous stairs.

'No! *Nooit!* Never! That's my Juanita! Who's she with, hey? *I swear . . .*'

Juanita made her *d'escalier* with *esprit*, though pyjamas with safety pins and teddy bears are not one with the décor. Even so, she is lovely in her self – dark flashing eyes and proud young carriage, head with massy hair held high. 'She walks in beauty as with starry skies . . .'

'Sheesh,' she says. 'Santa Maria! Pedro Bonito? *You?* I *skell* you out, you low bottom-feeding lobster! And as for you lot – yes, I see you there – I wish to goodness I could get just one night's decent sleep.'

BANG! The narrow lane shook and swayed and changed its shape. There was a sulphurous smell. And for their sins, the four fishermen found themselves in the night shelter down by the shunting yard. Ougat Wolf and Jan Piesang mumbled in their sleep and turned their backs. More blinking drunks to trouble us; what we come to then? 'As you make your bed so shall you lie upon it,' says Wolfie, champing on his hollow tooth.

From the harbour came the rumble of engines as the boats fired up for the early morning run. Fumes of diesel and power paraffin. *Star of the Sea*, *Marion Dawn*, *Maria Gomez, Hamidullah*, *Bonita My Lovely*, one by one the boats coughed, sputtered, and began their throbbing beat. The harbour lights winked, red and green, port and starboard, marking out the bullnose and the wider sea. The boats slid forth, rising and falling as they glided quick and neat upon the inky scene. Chokka, snoek and kabeljou may turn and quiver, but the prudent early crews will sail below their hunter's moon.

The longshoremen's barbershop quartet slept on. The sun, late as she was in early winter, rose, trailing clouds of glory from her wings. Over the bay she rose, bathing all in watery light. The first commuter trains ran past. In Simon's Town, ratings cleared their heads as they trudged back from liberty to minesweeper, frigate and corvette. Keen quartermasters of the morning watch were ready with watch list and bosun's call. Shopkeepers crept out to unshutter bottle store, boutique and bistro. Lovers heard the stern aubade – the watchman on the tower: 'Up! Thou rascal, rise, I see the dawning light; the night doth fly'. The muezzin was on his minaret. The railway clerk was in his booking office and the postman on his early round. The whitewashed day shone down upon the scene, and still the sleeping foursome snored. Juanita rose alone in wonder and went to look upon her renovated kitchen (granite tops).

'And as for that Pedro, Pedro Bonito, as for him, he can keep his dirty feet outside until he sobers up. Is the flounder happy in the jacuzzi, I wonder.'

'Knock knock.'

'Who's there?'

'Anna.'

'Anna who?'

'Me, Anna Persens. You up yet, Juanita?'

'Ey! Anna! Santa Maria, but you early! How you getting on?'

'Fine, fine. Sorry if I woke you – I came to get the first catch. Got a snoek at the harbour. Can you *vlek* it for me? What happened to your house? You doing alterations?'

Anna Persens, apprentice to the noted sangoma Malibongwe Ngingingini, was ushered in. She took her sharp-toothed snoek to the fancy kitchen.

'*Jirre!* You've done a lot since I've been here.'

'Ja. Bettering ourselves, you know.'

'Sure. Can I go to the bathroom?'

'Help yourself. Guest loo down the arcade. Second palm tree to the left.'

Anna found an enormous silver fish in the marbled whirlpool tub.

'You look simpatico,' said the flounder. 'Do me a favour. Get me outa here before Juanita changes her mind. I must go down to the sea again. Please? This whirlpool thing is bad as fabled Charybdis.'

Anna could have sworn the fish had spoken. And winked and dimpled at her as it spoke.

Persuasive one, it wooed her to its cause. Leaving the snoek, she slung the great flounder on her shoulder and returned to the vestibule.

'It's OK, Juanita! I've left it in the tub. I'll let myself out – Malibongwe's waiting for his breakfast. You go back to sleep.

See you soon.'

'OK, Anna! Bye-bye. Wish we could see you more.'

BANG! The sea, sky and sun wildly reeled about. For a moment everything went out of shape. And a ballpoint, with no human hand, scribbled in Juanita's new appointment book.

Anna left quietly with the flounder in her arms. This would be a meal for Malibongwe! Could do for two weeks – baked, or grilled, then fricasseed and curried. But the flounder had its own intentions. It peered round and up at her; a speculative and fishy eye.

'Psst,' it whispered. 'Easy does it. Now look – just between the two of us – you want three wishes too?'

THE PURPLE PANAMA

AUTUMN WAS CLAMPED DOWN ON CAPE TOWN with the power of a dowager's fist – elderly but alluring, decked with rich beauty, misty with veils.

Up in the leafy suburb of Gardens, Anita van Houwelingen opened the curtains of her musty flat. She preened herself, peered left, right, up and down into the mirror. She giggled, adjusted the purple panama at a rakish angle down over her long white face. Anita van Houwelingen had a date.

How did she know? Anita had read this. She had read it in the stars. She had delineated the sky the previous night: traced her transits, their orbs and aspects to her ascendant and descendant; to the mid-heaven and the *imum coeli*; the moon's nodes; the *caput* and the *cauda draconis*; the triplicities and quadruplicities. She had conjured, and she knew.

Across the city in the suburb of Green Point down near the shining sea, Fabricius de Kwaadsteniet gave a final tweak to his tie, brushed off invisible motes from the muted gloss of ostrich-skin espadrilles, glanced for the umpteenth time at the open page of his Loeb Virgil. Aeneas and Dido! An epic affair! (Fabricius de Kwaadsteniet was wont to fossick in his *Aeneid* for daily counsel.) So be it. He mildly sighed.

And forming the third point of a strange triangulation Malibongwe Ngingingini rose up naked from the mattress on the floor of his subsiding tenement in Salt River down by the railway workshops; rose up to his knees and raised his hands in the air and laughed in the shafts of morning sunlight. The *dolosse*, the bones, they have spoken! Today I shall take to me a bride.

Anna Persens cleaved to his naked chest; but he gently forced her off.

'No, my child. No. But stay with me and you shall see.'

Anna, as his apprentice, kept him supplied with *muti*, the organic matter that has magical and healing properties.

She scoured the corners of the city for herbs and unguents and galenicals, for tufts of feathers, claws and bones, for the skeletons or the stuffed or dressable torsos of little animals, dassies, birds, fish, and ostrich eggs, and iguanas, and platannas. And every month her task became more difficult as the city encroached on the vestiges of local fauna, as it encroached with insatiable mercantilism and consumed every stuffed creature, every last old stuffed and mounted fox or parrot or budgerigar gleaned from every attic.

Anna scoured rubbish dumps, the precincts of veterinary clinics, the SPCA; she made forays into second-hand shops in Long Street where she had to fight off pimps and skollies and idlers who mistook her for a girlfriend; she paid for tickets to visit the Natural History Museum, where she looked with deep and secret longing at the stuffed and mounted treasury of aardvarks, avocets and armadillos, eagles and hyenas, muishonds and molesnakes. She shivered with fierce delight as she wandered through the whale-well with its gargantuan skeletons and pendent carcasses. She loved Malibongwe dearly. Anna Persens would find him stuffed creatures, oh yes!

Anita van Houwelingen scooped up her miniature schnauzer Stoffel and put him in the handbag where he always travelled.

She stooped to lock her door, twitched her scented gloves, and smartly paced her way to the green enclave in the middle of the city, the Company's Gardens, where she would read the Saturday papers with her coffee.

Fabricius de Kwaadsteniet sighed a fastidious sigh. Dido? As a serious human proposition? He adjusted his bifocals and patted the spines of books to lodge them neatly.

Fabricius was an antiquarian and bibliophile, collector of classics and Africana. He turned over in his hand the catalogue from Clarens's, the rare book dealers in Long Street. Yes, indeed. There now and awaiting his inspection – the seventeenth-century original of Athanasius van Aarde's *Cartografie van 't Monomotapa*. Fabricius wiped away a touch of sudden drool. First Clarens's, then tea in the Gardens tearoom.

Anna Persens was as naked as her lover. She reluctantly let go of Malibongwe and wrapped a kikoi round her girlish thighs. She pulled on a T-shirt; looked back at him with her dark and secretive eyes; silently left the house.

He seeks a bride. Very well! Such a stuffed creature will I find today that he'll be moved to take me as bride instead. He'll never see the likes again. Such a creature will I find. First, the museum. Then the aviaries in the Gardens. And the shops in Long Street too. And the State Pathologist's; or right next door, the art school, sometimes they get in oddities for drawing classes. Anna massaged her deft fingers purposefully as she walked towards the city.

Overhead the autumn morning mists were lifting; birds swept up on columns of watery golden air. The world was washed in watercolours, bright as nuggets, full of weekend joy.

And invisible to the natural eye a drama was enacted in the southern skies: a rare and great epithalamion, the marriage of Venus and Mars, celestial counterparts to Dido and Aeneas, to Anita and Fabricius, to Anna and Malibongwe. A rare and powerful hymeneal syzygy, *conjunctio* between these most desirable of planetary bodies, and this located too within the passionate sign of Scorpio; and, host to these nuptials, the natural house of Taurus, home of sensual pleasures, and of things.

Small wonder that an instinct urge had taken hold upon the hearts and souls and flesh of these four – all of Cape Town felt this throb of autumn love.

Fabricius de Kwaadsteniet parked his puce BMW in Queen Victoria Street abreast of the Supreme Court, with suitable access both to the Gardens and to Long Street. Sniffing the promise on the morning air, he picked his eager way to Clarens's.

Patriarchal stones in the foundation courses of old buildings, wrought-iron grilles at basement level, pavement furniture of green-painted ironwork, newspaper banners, bicycles and mopeds chained to lampposts, yellow road-markings painted over ancient cobbles: these things delighted Fabricius, who had a sense of order that began with the absolute necessity of the world being correctly arranged up to the level of one's shins. It was his private fad to wear around his calves elastic suspenders for his socks. He shivered in a frisson of pleasure.

Anita van Houwelingen dipped her long and commanding nose into a cup of steaming java. She stretched out her legs beneath the demure modesty of her tweed skirts. She breathed deeply of the garden air, listened to the hum of voices in the tearoom, heard the flap of pigeons, the scuttling of feet, of squirrels, of leashed dogs. With her spoon she fed Stoffel biscuits dunked in coffee. She shook open the morning paper, found the horoscope, laughed through her teeth in silent scorn. She settled the purple panama more snugly on her head.

Malibongwe Ngingingini stretched luxuriously in the intoxicating air. The mild sun poured down from a gaping hole where wall and ceiling had collapsed. One day his suite of rooms would tumble right down below into the Parker brothers' pet food shop. (Faisal Parker believed that it would happen very soon. So be it.) He flexed his muscles with insouciant pleasure and took a breakfast swig from a bottle of buchu brandy. Let it be when he is lying with his bride! Then let the world fall down around their ears! For together they will cause the earth to shake and move. He grinned hugely to himself.

Fabricius was a disappointed man. His arch-rival Aidan Almost, canon of St Chrysostom's, had forestalled him – had bought the Van Aarde edition. Ah, well. In that case, tea. He picked his way back to the tearoom in the Gardens.

And there Fabricius noticed a commotion in a corner: a tall and elderly woman in a purple panama, struggling over something that was thrashing about in her handbag – a trio of waitresses in hysterics – one or two helpless customers bobbing at her busy elbows.

'Madam, may I be of assistance?'

'My dog – my Stoffel – Oh me! He's caught in the zip of my handbag! He'll suffocate! Please help me to unfasten him!'

Anita van Houwelingen's morning was ruined. She grappled with her handbag, with the squirming and squealing form of Stoffel, with the fountain of odds and ends, hairnets, clips and combs, bits and bobs, tickets and cards and lipstick and pencils and phials of cologne and lozenges and cachoux and loose change spraying out in the coffee-laden air.

Anna Persens looked on darkly through a fringe of palm fronds. She concentrated on the scene with the intensity of a hungry hunter. So far she had drawn a blank. All she could think of was to buy a fresh snoek at Texeira's fishery and give it to Malibongwe for lunch stuffed with apricots and garlic.

But now the sight of the schnauzer Stoffel was as balm in

Gilead. What would be the outcome of that struggle in the handbag on the tearoom table?

Oh no! The man with glasses and the jacket and the fancy cravat is taking the whole show with him – they're leaving, handbag and dog and all. But I'm going with them, Anna made up her mind with clear decision. She picked up the purple panama, which had fallen from Anita van Houwelingen's head, and filled it with the broadcast contents of the bag. She ran after the elderly pair, got into the back of the puce BMW, and they didn't think to challenge her.

Fabricius drove furiously through the city to his town house. He had a notion that he might free the schnauzer with his set of miniature instruments for the repair and tooling of Andalusian leather.

Anna Persens hung on in the back seat of the careering car and rearranged the kikoi around her naked thighs. She was immersed in thought. On one hand, if prepared properly the dog might prove an adequate specimen for Malibongwe. On the other, Anna was fond of pets and hoped that Stoffel could yet be released from the zip. And again, it was against the code of the sangoma to use for *muti* any creature that had been attached to man. Anna shrugged. Too bad. He'll have to settle for a snoek.

They pulled up in Loader Street, Fabricius's fashionable address. They hastened into his townhouse.

'Give him me,' said Anna Persens. 'I've often done this trick before. I need a pair of tweezers and a tin of three-in-one oil.' From time to time she'd had to free her master from his trouser flies.

To assuage Anita's anxiety, Fabricius steered her towards the library to inspect his etchings and books.

'Oh! Oh my! That surely isn't Henry Cornelius Agrippa von Nettesheim's *De Occulta Philosophia*?'

'Indeed,' answered Fabricius with measured pride. 'The first edition, Antwerp, 1533.'

'My dear Fabricius!' murmured Anita, thoroughly at home. 'And look! Robertus Fluvius' *Utriusque Cosmi Historia*! Oh! Oh me! And is not that the manuscript of the *Chymical Wedding* by Christian Rosencreuz?'

Anita found herself pressing against Fabricius lest she swoon down to the floor. Fabricius snapped his elastic garters in unaccustomed agitation.

'It is done!' called Anna Persens from the study. 'Stoffel is now free!'

And Anna wandered into the library after the leaping little dog. And then she saw – animals! Stuffed and mounted animals! Oh, Malibongwe my darling, if you could only set your eyes on these!

Ranged around the room on pedestals and under glass domes were the most extraordinary creatures Anna had ever seen. There were auks and dodos and a coelacanth, and hippogriffs and basilisks and giraffes. Even the rare manticore and wolpertinger, and tiny winged asphyxes. Anna had to shake her head to clear her thoughts.

'Oh, Stoffel my sweetie! Come to me, my cupid, my precious!'

'Thank you for releasing this lady's pet. How may I repay you?'

Anna swelled with joy. Wordlessly she pointed out a hippogriff. Fabricius reached up and placed the creature in her arms. She grinned and bobbed and left the two of them to calm the schnauzer down.

Anna ran all the way to Salt River with the purple panama stuck on her head and the hippogriff lodged in her arms. She ran up the swaying stairs to Malibongwe's rooms. She called out and flourished the stuffed creature at him.

Malibongwe looked up in blank astonishment. *Ewe!* Oh, yes yes yes! A hippogriff! Anna's found a hippogriff! O rare and potent *muti!* 'Hau! *Ndiyakuthanda*, darling Anna! I love you!'

And Anna Persens flung herself at Malibongwe Ngingingini and they fell down onto his bed. And then there came a slow and mighty rumbling; and a maelstrom of weary mortar, friable brick, rotten wood. And when the dust had settled, there stood up from the shambles that lay in Faisal and Abdurahman Parker's pet food shop a naked and grinning pair of lovers, he with a winged hippogriff held aloft in his triumphant hands and she with a purple panama perched pertly on her head.

ELEPHANT'S BREATH

Main Road, Wynberg, is a long and scoliotic spine that runs for two kilometres down the paunchy torso of this old suburb. You pass the old Curzon Cinema (now an auctioneers) and the Dutch Reformed cemetery, down past any number of bustling chain stores, and the balconied and pilastered shopfronts of a century ago, with their flyblown haberdasheries and book exchanges and appliance-repair stores; and then comes motorland, where blocks of colonial gothic have been levelled for shadecloth-covered car lots.

On the way you pass a place where there used to be a tramway terminus when the trolleybuses ran on the route from Wynberg to Cape Town, trolleybuses on rubber tyres and hooked up to the overhead trolleylines like electric elephants with slender trunks raised on high – and before them, the trams. Gay posters hanging on the lampposts advertise Bodrum's Magic Circus, which will parade through the city on the morrow. Here you find a green-and-purple-painted mosque, and next to it Solly Rubin's second-hand furniture emporium that spills imbuia bureaux and divans and office chairs onto the pavement, and Qonde's *muti* shop, and tucked in beside these a tiny frontage with a sign that reads 'Charles Edgeworth, Rare Books'.

What, you wonder, is that known feral person, Anna Persens (called the Subaltern by her women's group), apprentice and almost-inducted lover of the Woodstock sangoma Malibongwe Ngingingini, doing in 'Charles Edgeworth, Rare Books'? It is nearly five on a Friday afternoon fully two weeks to the end of the month, and surely it is time to lock up and go home; time for shoppers and casual browsers to catch the train; time for the Subaltern to take her anti-retrovirals and make Malibongwe's meal and pour his beer for him. The muezzin at the Al Baraka mosque is already calling the faithful to their prayers, 'Praise be to God, Lord of the Worlds, the Compassionate, the Merciful, King of the Day of Judgment.'

But there appears to be an argument inside the cramped and ill-lit interior of 'Charles Edgeworth, Rare Books'.

'Not a cent less than fifty rands will I take. I'm closing the till – look – this is your last chance, Anna; I'm going home.'

'Thirty.' Anna does not bandy words.

'Fifty, I say. Get out. Anna, you waste my time – that's fine ivory. You buy it for fifty and you'll be to the good.'

With her large brown eyes and girlish figure, in a T-shirt with Ndebele-style patterns, a denim jacket the colour of elephant's breath, cut like a hussar's dolman, and a cotton skirt with little mirrors sewn into the pleats, the Subaltern crushed to her breast the patinated yellow billiard ball. She knew her man – she knew Cy Koentz of old, this appraiser, this magpie with the shining eye, proprietor of the pseudonymous 'Charles Edgeworth, Rare Books', a calculating man who once drove into a desert monastery a Cairo Coptic antiquarian who thought he'd never meet his match. There had never been a Charles Edgeworth. The shop was opened in 1903 by a Jewish refugee from Prague, who in the climate of the time deemed it better to adopt an Anglo name for purposes of trade; and as for Cy Koentz's own credentials – but that's another story.

Cy's glint followed Anna's wrist to where the billiard ball nestled coyly. Anna held her tongue and returned a limpid gaze. She had to have the billiard ball. She knew it was old and those hairline cracks would open, and it would start to flake; she knew it was worth no more than thirty rands; but there was no time to argue. Silently she passed Cy Koentz a russet-coloured fifty-rand note. The antiquarian shot her an appraising and triumphant glance and turned to close up shop.

Late-autumn leaves dithered where three stunted plane trees forced their trunks through the tarmac pavement. The evening sky over Castle Rock glowed with confused cloud shapes; the wind eddied, an equinoctial cocktail of contrary ripples. Anna shivered in her denim jacket and was glad of the bottle of Old Brown sherry in her bag, against which the billiard ball gently knocked. Tonight she and Malibongwe would celebrate. The ivory ball was a special commission from him; this night he would demonstrate to her his use for it. And tomorrow morning there'd be a circus parade! Anna shivered again, this time in glee. She loved the musty fragrance of the animals, the heady music, the grease-painted clowns, the acrobats and tumblers. There would be a Gypsy King and Queen in royal raiment, riding in a palanquin of pure Bohemian crystal.

Meanwhile in the gathering dusk three silent *bergies* wrestled a supermarket trolley down Church Street. Past the Anglican and Methodist cemeteries they toiled, past the Odd Fellows' Hall, heading for the Main Road. Their leader, Ougat Wolf, strained against their overburdened cart as it listed on the camber of the street. Jammed into it was the skeleton of a mule they were taking to Oom Hein Wagner down in Ottery. Oom Hein Wagner paid cash for bone, which he ground up into his own bestselling recipe for plant food. It was a long way yet for them this evening, out to the flower farms and market gardens of Ottery on the fringes of the Cape Flats.

Where they found the skeleton of the mule there is no knowing. The Subaltern stared and shrugged her shoulders as they rattled on in the gloom. As apprentice to the sangoma it usually fell to her to find organic remains, or *muti*. The skeleton of a mule is rare trove indeed. She pursed her lips and clutched her parcel with the billiard ball and sherry. She headed for the station and took a train back to Woodstock, to Malibongwe Ngingingini's newly repaired tenement above

Faisal and Abdurahman Parker's pet food shop down near the railway workshops.

'Sharp, my darling Anna! *Ndiyakuthanda!* How I love you, *intombi yam*,' Malibongwe, all expansive, greeted her as she held out the yellowed ivory orb. 'I knew you'd find it for me. Give it here.' He took the ball between thumb and index finger and peered at it in the candlelight of his studio. She poured two tumblers of sherry. When Malibongwe was working he fell into a trance of concentration. He had to have his supper now before he was lost to her, to appetite, to the outer world. But his back was turned; he was already deep in the pages of a thick and dusty book – a volume Anna recognised in the flickering light as having come in a parcel not long ago from Cy Koentz, proprietor of Charles Edgeworth, Rare Books. Malibongwe muttered as he flipped the pages; he hummed a low-keyed ditty; he chanted snatches of verse which might be ancient Ethiopian, might be Coptic, might – for all Anna knew – be Aramaic or Gujarati or Catalan. A light autumnal air scurried across the floor of the dark studio. Anna shrugged, quaffed her sherry, and curled up on the bed with an old copy of *Fairlady*.

Ougat Wolf and his two friends earned fifty rands from Oom Hein for the mule skeleton. It was nearly ten at night when they knocked on the back door of Kaisersaschern, his isolated homestead, but he was in a generous mood. As the trolley and its lugubrious burden trundled through his bed of mustard lettuce, and the awkward frame of that sad mule came tumbling through his open door, he leashed his lean and hideous dogs and sent the three rejoicing on their way. Oom Hein drew the pile of bones into his workshop, flicked on the light, tied a butcher's blue apron around his bulky figure, and slowly and laboriously fed them into his patent crusher. Midnight came and still his light was on, still the diesel motor of the crusher growled its monotonous and sullen note. Bag after thick brown paper bag of bestselling fertiliser was piled in the farther recess of Oom Hein Wagner's capacious wood-and-iron workshop.

Only after he had gone to bed, some time near two in the morning, did four shadowy masked figures slip down his sandy drive past the sunflower patch, past the rusty John Deere tractor, and (giving the old homestead a wide berth for the sleeping dogs) find their way to the workshop where a pile of twenty bags of fertiliser awaited them. The dark figures flitted to and fro until all the bags were gone, loaded in the back of their van. Leaving an envelope with money tacked onto the shed wall ('*Köszönöm*,' it said, which is Hungarian for 'Thank you'), they melted into the reaches of Varkensvlei and Schaapkraal, their passage marked by only the faintest whiff of bonemeal phosphates.

Back in Woodstock, Malibongwe Ngingingini finally turned from his books, stretched, and shook his apprentice. 'Anna, are you awake? It's time. I need your help.' He was dressed in a pair of gumboots and a khaki-yellow housecoat. 'Bring the bucket, please. I need to get some soil from the yard.' The two of them descended the swaying flight of stairs down from Malibongwe's tenement into the walled yard at the rear. 'Try not to make too much noise,' he whispered. He didn't want his mongrel, Nostril, woken at this late hour. What he had to do would not brook the dog's playful curiosity.

The waxing moon cast a velvety refulgence on the pair as they sifted soil into the bucket behind a frangipani tree. 'That should do it,' he nudged Anna. 'I don't suppose it matters if there's some fertiliser in the soil. Might help, in fact. Might be homoeopathic. Quickly now, back upstairs. Soon it will be dawn.' Indeed the hour was nearly four, and Malibongwe fought down a stirring of anxiety. Whenever a certain task was laid upon him he knew he had to face it; but he reassured himself that he'd be given the means to fulfil his purpose. Fortitude and a steady hand would see his preparations done in time. He did, however, ask the Subaltern to pour him out a modest glass of sherry. It was cold and his hands felt stiff.

Anna watched as Malibongwe distributed the soil evenly onto a sheet of plastic on the naked floorboards. 'I need a potent power this day,' he said. 'I need a fortress, a force, a leviathan. You shall see.' He patted the soil into the rough profile of an elephant. 'Which has the bigger ears,' Anna asked herself as she watched, 'African, or Indian?' Delicately Malibongwe defined the silhouette of the loamy beast. He too hesitated over the ears, but only for a moment. He got up off his knees and took off his housecoat and the boots. He adorned his body with ornaments of porcupine and cowry shell, with copper bracelets and torques, with beads and amulets of wood and leather and glass and painted clay.

'Now then, Anna,' Malibongwe warned her, 'what's to be done has not been essayed for four centuries. The last man to do what I must do was the Bohemian Jehudah ben Bezalel, known as Rabbi Loew of Prague, four hundred years ago; and it has never been attempted on this continent. Listen, look, and stay silent.'

The sangoma stretched, flailed his arms like a windmill, and leaped into a circular dance. Around and about the prostrate form of the elephant he whirled, and as he whirled he chanted and cried out. 'Earth!' he cried, 'and Air, and elemental Fire, Water too, inhabit ye this elephant, this image, this – this – entity.' As he danced he tossed small things onto the elephant: a dried gecko, drops of distilled water, the dregs of the sherry glass, showers of sparks from his Zippo until the flint broke up. His bare feet pounded the boards until the bell jars and the bookcases around the wainscot jingled and rocked. He grabbed a battered bugle, raised it to his lips and blasted a clarion note. Anna flinched – surely Nostril would be woken up; and sure enough, his urgent bark now joined the rising frenzy in the room.

The false dawn streaked with faintest pallid green the eastern sky above the Hottentots Holland and Great Drakenstein. Seabirds winged over Woodstock Beach, and the rumble of an early train rattled the still-curtained casements of houses in the railway suburbs of Rosebank, Mowbray, Observatory and Salt River. In the remnants of the night a solitary vehicle headed towards the city. It drove cautiously, avoiding highways, keeping to the cover of small and slumbering side streets. Its number plates were masked with tape, even as the four occupants wore dark woollen balaclavas pulled full over their faces. A faint whiff of phosphates hung about them as they came. They reached the central city, where with practised ease they reversed up an alley, exited their van by the rear, and scaled a whitewashed eight-foot wall. Cautiously they hauled a hessian sack up after them. They made their way onto the sealed-off balcony of an old four-storey building which was due for demolition. From this rickety vantage they surveyed the length of Darling Street and, facing them, the expanse of the Grand Parade. They would have a clear view of the coming procession. From its plinth among the palm trees that fringe the Parade, the portly granite form of King Edward the Seventh gazed back blandly in the gathering dawn.

Malibongwe sweated heavily as he swayed trancelike over what appeared to be an inflating greyish-brown football. Anna stared in awe, while she held Nostril by his collar. The football swelled, and swelled. It had a head, a fat and growing torso, a little tuft of a tail. From four corners of the ballooning torso waved stout legs. A trunk like a tentacle popped out from the head; short coarse hair bristled along the ridges of the body. 'Quick, Anna! The billiard ball!' Malibongwe cried. Nostril whimpered. Anna frantically cast about for the ivory billiard ball. 'Hurry! And pass me my Koki pen too.'

He was nearly done in – covered with perspiration, exhausted from his all-night efforts, anxiety pressing upon him as the first blush of sunrise came into his room. He covered the billiard ball with glyphs and characters, cabbalistic ciphers culled from the notes of Rabbi Loew. "Now!' he cried, 'Stand fast! Hold Nostril tight. On no account let him loose.'

The sangoma raised the yellowed ivory orb on high, then plunged it down and lodged it in the mouth of his jumbo golem.

'*Ndlovu!*' he cried, in a great voice. '*Ndlovu, phefumla ume ngeenyawo!* Arise, O Elephant, breathe and arise, I conjure you!' For what seemed an eternity there was silence in the room. The big fat football swayed with the billiard in its mouth and seemed set to float up off the floor. Malibongwe's dark eyes flashed in concentration. Anna held back the straining Nostril. Again the sangoma cried out, '*Ndlovu! Ndlovu! Phefumla ume ngeenyawo!*'

And then it started. The football swelled and heaved, its flanks began to twitch, its trunk waved, fine long tusks pushed out where the billiard ball was lodged, its feet scrabbled for purchase on the floor. It grew and grew. 'Hau! It's working! Stand back! Look out, the floor is going! Save my precious autochrone!' All too late Malibongwe realised that he should have made his golem in the yard. The great elephant rose up from its knees and Malibongwe's apartment shuddered. The ceiling came down in a mess of lath and plaster and spider nests. 'Hold onto the elephant! It's our only chance!' So Anna clung to the great beast's neck, struggling with the twisting form of Nostril under her arm. Malibongwe hung onto the other side. With a rending crash the floor of his apartment gave in and the beast with its cargo plunged down into Faisal and Abdurahman Parker's pet food shop. The elephant shook itself and nuzzled dog biscuits while Malibongwe's household tumbled about their ears.

Malibongwe cleared his mind. 'Too bad,' he said with rue. 'Right now, we have a job ahead. There's no time to be lost, I hear the circus music.'

Indeed, Anna could make out the rousing din of the Radetzky March – the circus was coming! Down Albert Road it came.

Malibongwe settled himself up on the elephant like a mahout, squatting cross-legged behind its great head, almost enfolded in its ears. He gave Anna a hand up, and she sat behind him with Nostril in her arms. He still wore his feathers and amulets, and Anna her thin cropped hussar dolman the colour of elephant's breath. 'On,' he cried. 'Mush, mush! Forward!'

Ndlovu swayed, tossed some debris from his flanks, and rhythmically moved, trumpeting, down Locomotive Close to Albert Road.

There a motley sight met their eyes – the circus parade! Bodrum's Magic Circus! – headed by outriders on palomino geldings, with nubile gymnasts vaulting and springing behind, a troupe of clowns tripping and sprawling as they came, gay wheeled cages in which reposed majestic beasts of veld and fable, a marching band, a maiden with a unicorn, trapeze artistes in spangled tights, and sailors dancing hornpipes. The fire-eater dashed fiercely by in a blue nimbus of methylated spirits; Samson in his leopard skins and the bearded lady marched proudly arm in arm. The band broke into Hungarian dances, and round the corner twirled fifty dragomans with jaunty beards and sparklers. Behind them in a dazzling light of shining crystal came the Gypsy King and Queen, Prozacz and Rosalie, their debut on the continent of Africa. With proud flashing eyes and bejewelled gestures they acknowledged the ragged cheers of urchins and commuters. Behind the gypsy entourage came Ougat Wolf and friends with supermarket trolleys and sacks of empty bottles, arguing and jigging to the music and full deeply pulling at a *swartvarkie* of Oom Tas. In the rear ran the dogs, Nostril's gang, a motley pack drawn by the exotic reek of panther, ostrich, giraffe and elephant.

Malibongwe, Anna, Nostril and their mount merged unremarked into the parade. They trundled with the throng towards the city and Darling Street. Streamers of all hues were tossed about. The band broke into 'Nkosi Sikelel' iAfrika'. The procession came abreast of the City Hall and the Grand Parade, and then, and *then* – Malibongwe felt the ancient voice of Rabbi Jehudah ben Bezalel in his inner ear: 'The time has come! Great peril impends! Look to the Gypsy King! King Prozacz and his bride!'

Malibongwe broke into a sweat. What to do? Whence will the peril come? What form does it take? Again the voice vibrated in his ear: 'Look to the balcony on your left. Opposite the statue of the stout monarch. On the balcony, grave danger. Sulphur and – and – phosphate are there. Attend the King! Steer your beast to save the King!'

Malibongwe glanced to his left. He saw four shadowy masked figures rise from the balcony and sway aloft a huge round smoking form, saw them draw back as if to throw this device into the nearing palanquin. His mind calculated and he cried: 'Anna, leap off! Take Nostril and get behind the statue!' Now he faced the mammoth beast towards the balcony. He faced the hooded figures and charged them on his lumbering mount. They panicked, slipped and fell in haste, and the smoking great device rolled from their nerveless grasp. It hit the pavement. Malibongwe flung himself from his speeding golem and curled up in the gutter. With a flaming roar and the kick of a mule the phosphate bomb went off, bringing down the balcony, spilling its singed and murderous occupants into a mess of shattered shop fittings and dustbins. Malibongwe's magic beast took the blast and, with an aftershock of elephantine afflatus, shattered into a thousand atoms.

'Am I never free of peril?' cried King Prozacz, breaking the stunned silence. 'From continent to continent they chase me. Subjects that murmur and seek my ruin, they cease not in their scheming.' Queen Rosalie embraced him, and Anna came up, trembling, to offer help – aspirins, a swig of Old Brown, sticking plasters, and safety pins for their torn raiment.

'How can we thank you?' the Gypsy King and Queen asked Malibongwe and the Subaltern. '*Köszönöm*, *köszönöm*, brave friends.' The dragomans rushed up, bristled their whiskers, and fiercely cheered in Finno-Ugric.

Anna watched a solitary yellow billiard ball pitch and bounce away. It cannoned off a parked car and into the Criterion Bar and Pool Room. Malibongwe squeezed her hand and silently thanked Rabbi Loew of Prague and Cy Koentz of Charles Edgeworth, Rare Books.

'Snookered,' he said with quiet satisfaction.

WHITED SEPULCHRES

Toby's brow was wrinkled. Toby Graaff, archaeologist and heritage consultant, held his heart and mind in balance. Which was lighter? Which weighed him more? What pressure points, what chakras, what resonances of the soul and body held the twain in counterpoise? Was one real and one mere shadow-play? He shrugged away the moody thought and turned back to the graveyard and its antique stones.

This was one of a neighbourhood of graveyards down the backs of churches in Church Street in the old village (now a Cape Town suburb) of Wynberg. Wynberg held a dense layering of memory for historical archaeologists.

There was the village core, the sheds where blacksmiths and farriers once toiled, the carters, grain merchants, hardwaremen and Lithuanian haberdashers. There were Cornish masons, Muslim flower sellers, washerwomen, and towards the hill the winding streets of thatched stone or whitewashed cottages where once lived the British officers and their wives. These clustered around Waterloo Green and Wellington Avenue named in honour of the Iron Duke.

Then came the broad estates that ran up Wynberg Hill towards the glowing mountainside – Victorian piles with towers, conservatories, arboretums, coachhouses, iron gates and leafy avenues, built by mining magnates and by lords and ladies in those days of moneyed grace and Raj.

Church, State, Crown and Army – Wynberg had its share, and the churches were a hologram of social class: St John's stone Norman nave among the shady oaks upon the hill for the Establishment, the flower of Albion's colonial chivalry; the capacious Methodist for nonconformist NCOs and Cornishmen; a wedding cake of Dutch Reformed white Gothic for the Afrikaans and Dutch; and tucked around the corner its now-redundant mini-me, the modest whitewashed mission church for kitchen-Dutch, the humbler folk with more than just a touch of tarbrush (that nasty old phrase) in their genes. And the earnest Lithuanians and Ashkenazim built their grand synagogue for housing of the holy Torah, while solemn Islam was below the railway line, a stone's throw from the Dominicans. There from his minaret the muezzin sang out the call to daily prayers.

The Carmelites in mystic silence were another breed and followed their vows next door to the parish of St John, among the wooded uplands where rustling leaves and murmur of doves assuaged the cloistered heart. And down Waterloo Green, the Lutheran Deutsche Kirche burned the flame of Reformation. Baptists and Plymouth Brethren made their fiery stand with foot-pump harmoniums on the Town Hall steps or beside the Railway Hotel, where souls of travelling salesmen were in peril of hard tack. Wynberg village was well served, and this besides the Ancient and Accepted Rites, the Netherlandish, Scottish, English and Irish Lodges, and the Odd Fellows and their ilk.

And Time, fobbed or longcased or gold-honoured or carriage-clocked, set all this down in regimental history and parish record, in journal and in register, in road name and name of terrace or villa, and in legacies of heart and mind and soul. And most of all it set this down in leaden letters in the slate and marble and the granite of the graveyards, where Time was very busy in the war of 1899. Lancer, private, gunner, carbineer from around the gilded empire lay in Wynberg soil, and made peace with Cape Dutch patriots and farming families who slumbered there beside them.

Enough to burden any archaeologist, let alone the akashic record. And how these dusty ones impinged upon the living

– Ougat Wolf and Jan Piesang were too *bang* to make their bed among sad cypresses, and preferred the noisy night shelter in the old Salvation Army chapel. Schoolchildren going to catch the train swapped ghoul stories as they took the shortcut through the dusty graves. But now there were plans to deconsecrate the Dutch Reformed graveyard and sell it off; and Toby Graaff had work to do before this happened.

The trouble was a sculptured angel. Her soft features, her clear brow and fine sweet nose and lips all made Toby think of Clementina. He was here to save that angel – save her and all the speckled monuments of time that lay beneath her shapely marble wings. A long and tedious task of simple record-making. Round him in the churchyard the white butterflies dithered like confetti; whitewashed tombs, the iron railings around the family plots, these wore under the dusty African sun the weariness of long-habituated marriage beds: the coverlets, the iron bedsteads, the forlorn singletons and the grand kingsize ones, their lustre long dulled by whitewashed sunlight and unkempt grass and rust. Empty jam jars and broken pots among the grass where flowers had been set; and the lone dark stone pine, broad syringa, dusty-pink oleander, and the brick-red of ramping bougainvillea that grew despite all this, and only helped to point the vanity of life.

'Vanity of vanities, all is vanity, saith the Preacher. That which hath been will be, and there is nothing new under the sun.'

Thus, old Johannes Jacobus Hermanus van Driel and his lone headstone – seen it all, and to be seen again another day. Jacoba Petronella Maria Coerecius and husband and five children in their wide bed; she did what she could, Toby thought wryly, and this to be done again and yet again by generations still to come.

'Gezaaid in zwakheid, opgewekt in kracht,' said the cast-iron lettering in the iron archway: 'Sown in weakness, raised in strength.'

What was biting Toby Graaff? Is this what comes of working in a graveyard, this unaccounted metaphysics? The whited sepulchres seemed to him to speak of mere display – a kind of sad acting, hypocrisy perhaps (which meant, in the Greek, performance on the stage). Just that, acting out a kind of life while empty at the core. The stone angel smiled and reached out and poked him in the midriff; in the third chakra, to be precise.

'Hey! Who did that?' Toby spun around too late to see the fading marbled grin.

The cemetery was silent in the afternoon sun save for a gentle dove in the unkempt old syringa tree and one bee that fussed at autumn daisies. The muted hum of traffic on Church Street was the only sound that spoke of present time. Toby might have stood in time suspended – except that in days gone past there would have been an elder, or a widow with a trowel and seedlings, the sexton, or the dominee himself. Now the outer world was hemmed in behind the oleanders by great rolling tides of convolvulus that grew up on the iron arch and reached out even to the angel on her plinth. And time itself was hemmed in by the sense of déjà vu.

Toby shook his head and sat down on a gravestone. He took out his notebook and his pen. Nobody really cared, but the graveyard was to be sold and a petrol station built instead. Nobody came to tend the graves, but the South African National Heritage Resources Act of 1999 did say that burial sites and cemeteries must be surveyed prior to disturbance. Toby was engaged to do a full survey of all the graves, the worthier of the stonework, and every name and legend on the headstones. These would be re-sited elsewhere, with all the mortal remains. Dusty work, he thought.

And he wasn't in the mood for this. An unaccustomed moodiness was on his heart, a torpor, whether melancholia or taedium vitae, inertia or lack of vitamins, or longueurs or ennui or good old-fashioned sloth. Into his head came the picture of a woodcut by Albrecht Dürer: a fallen angel, heavy-bodied, slumped head on hands among a pile of geometrical shapes, pondering a book; all the signs of learning about it – but no light. 'Melencolia' it was called. Science without meaning, reason without soul, mind without heart, the dull sublunary world hemmed in with useless learning. And beside this angel on a wall there hung a bell; and next to that a magic square, a number game: sixteen numbers squared up in blocks, and whichever way you added them you reached the selfsame sum – vertically, horizontally, diagonally, they teased your reason by their insistent answer. All things come to the same in the end. 'Vanity of vanities, saith the Preacher.'

'Pthh.'

'Ey?'

'Ptooi!'

Someone spat, and a bright orange berry from the broad syringa landed on his notebook's open page.

He shook his head again and brushed it off. This was the very place for moodiness, here where the old theology gave its forms to art. The angel on her plinth was surely from the 1890s, at the height of pre-Raphaelite enthusiasm and its popular evangelical uses: gently animated, both sexy and modest and beautiful and teasing-moody in its brooding pouting girlish face. Would she (it must be she) have a bellybutton? He thought of photographs he had seen from that period, women in thick black skirts, buttoned up against the heat of Africa, dumpy in their layered heavy clothes, mostly hard-featured as they squared up to the camera. And occasionally a striking smiling face, that seemed to have escaped, if only for the moment, from the epoch's dour mood. But they couldn't all have been so dour, and they had bellybuttons and soft bodies under all those clothes, and after all this angel was quite something. Might have been an adventuress, an artist's model, a soubrette, a babe of note.

A great flapping, as of wings, and disturbance in the air that made his notebook's pages rustle. What was that? The dove sat still upon its perch. What went past? Was it a guinea fowl or hadeda or Egyptian goose? The heavy silent air was broken for an instant – and then once again the still, oppressive autumn heat.

Toby fell asleep. His notebook dropped to the dry grass. He dreamed.

He found himself in a land of light. Clementina, who occupied his waking thoughts but not his home and bed, looked at him from her shiny plinth. Ah, the bellybutton! She let go the pole that seemed to give her height, and swung down at him and brushed her long hair from her face and blew a kiss. And then she swung back up again and turned away.

He struggled in a land of dark. Dark hair brushed his cheek and light laughter went skittering away to deeper silence. He stretched out to find his path and felt cold stone.

He passed through lands of empty veld where dry voices called for water. Khaki drill, hot serge, leather and cracked bugles.

He opened a door to rich orchards where peacocks preened and honeybirds darted among blossom. A black crow flew at him and chased him back.

He climbed a winding stair and at the top the burning tower smelt of gardenia and hot roses.

She took him by the hand and rushed him to the attic, where a bright-coloured coffin lay on trestles. Bang! It flew out of the gable window into the starry night. She rushed him down the stairs and there they all were waiting, laughing, dancing, singing to the stars.

They marched the slow march by his side, the drum beat slowly and the horses trod before the mourning carriage and the black-draped hearse. Children skipped beside and wondered.

Shabbily clad labourers dug and dug, and their sharp spades poked his ribcage and tickled him. They teased him out with poles and shovels. 'Is this *your* angel?' they asked. 'Is *your* name written there?' 'Where's the record, man?' 'Who took her photograph?' 'Is it true? You assume too much,' they accused him. 'Why don't you act?'

He couldn't move. He had no power, no volition and no vital force. They shovelled him into some other place among the dry bones all around. And down they pressed with giant stones, and one, like unto a sculptured angel, pressed on his heart and kissed him on the lips.

Toby woke with a start, both panic and sunlight in his head. The dove had left the syringa tree, but the bee still buzzed among the daisies. He picked up his notebook and looked around. Enough of this, he thought to himself. I need a break. I'll come back tomorrow and get this job done then.

'Are you all right? You know what to do now, don't you?'

'Who's that?' he asked. (A soft voice whispering in his ear.) 'Who is it?'

The angel sighed, flapped her wings together, and spoke more firmly: 'You need to get your act together, Toby Graaff.'

'But I *said* I'd come back tomorrow. Really tired, not in the mood now, got to go.'

Toby's mind and heart were mingled all together. He was light-headed, heavy-hearted, dull-minded, devil-may-care. A talking angel. Yes, sure, the stones all have stories to be told. I need a holiday. Must I record what this angel says? Where's my pen? Am I going mad? Have I got flu or what?

'Sit down and listen to me.' She had a compelling soft voice. He obeyed and sat on a fallen gravestone.

'So. You are an archaeologist of some ability.'

He waited.

'Yes? And you know a lot about the past, and all these' – she swept her hand around the graveyard – 'these monuments and sad memorials.'

'Um. Yes.'

'And you are born and bred here, are you not? Where are your own people buried?'

Toby spoke back, half against his will. 'I'm a South African, yes. Born in Cape Town. If you must know, my people came here three centuries ago from Holland. And from England on my mother's side. White South African for what that signifies, a bit of Portuguese too on my paternal grandmother's side, all in the record for anyone to see. Check the birth and death certificates in the Master's Office if you want.'

'So you've got some spirit, have you? That's something. I'm not contesting your credentials. And these generations of yours are sleeping in this African soil. I bet I got a few sisters standing over some of them. Mine here's a toff of some sort, Buckinghamshire Fusiliers, Captain Sir Jasper de la Court, poor sod. How ever did he come to get a plot in the Dutch Reformed cemetery? Not his turf at all.'

'I've got no idea where my people are buried.'

'Some archaeologist. Never mind. As you said yourself, all is vanity. Do you like my looks?'

The angel tossed her head, flicked her curly hair. Toby glanced around him.

'Just a moment. As you rightly say, this is a Dutch Reformed cemetery. You should be speaking Dutch, or Afrikaans perhaps. And you shouldn't be so vain. You're supposed to be a Calvinist angel.'

'All right then. Let's put things into little boxes, shall we? Ask Sir Jasper what *he's* doing here. Want to check my bellybutton too?'

Toby chuckled. This was something else. A talking Calvinist angel with gender, a demimondain face, and attitude.

'Come on, modernise,' said the angel. 'Let's get real.'

'Er?'

'You, you spend far too much energy among antiques. I know you've got a job to do, and I know it's important to preserve us and keep a sense of heritage. For sure. But listen, guy, how old are you? You're too young to be a curator or whatever, and you're not young enough to be innocent and dumb. Know what I mean?'

'What you mean?'

'Duh. You've been staring at me ever since you got here this morning, dear. Check out my wings, sweetheart.' The angel pouted and flapped. 'Sorry about all this drapery, bet you'd like to see my figure better.' With a practised Pre-Raphaelite hand she smoothed the folds around her breasts and down over her good hips.

'And because why? Why have you been eyeing me like that? Don't answer if you don't want. I know anyway.'

Toby reddened against his will.

'You think I look like the one that you like, isn't it, Toby?'

'Umm.'

'OK, OK! I'm flattered. I'll explain. I was expecting you. Yesterday there was this other woman I met. Carrying a big fish. She was young, some would say pretty in her own dark way, intense. So she was wearied with this massive fish and she sat down here to rest. She used the tap over there to get the fish some water. Fish was alive. Are you listening?'

Toby nodded.

'You think it's peculiar that I can talk? Lol. You should have heard that fish.'

Toby passed his hand across his eyes.

'The fish could talk, Toby Graaff! Nineteen to the dozen. Donkey's hind leg off. "Woman, wherefore do you bear me to this dry and barren place? Woman, kindly wipe my eye. Woman, if that's chlorinated water I'll have you know a flounder merits better. Why do we have to go by minibus taxi, good woman; I would ride in finer fashion being magical and all. How far is it to where we're going, forsooth?" and on and on and on.

'"Sheesh," says the dark young woman, "you say I can have three wishes, let's get on with it. If I wasn't such a softy we'd be home in Woodstock by now and you'd be in the oven. You're a lucky fish! I've brought you here because it's nice and private. Do your thing, and then I promise you, flounder, we go straight to Muizenberg beach and you go back into the sea."

'"Very well, good woman," replies this fish, "let's do it. Make your wishes even now."

'So the young woman – girl, I suppose, almost – she thinks. She sits and strokes the fish and thinks: How hard is it to make a wish, I ask myself. Like I mean, just how hard can it be to come up with ideas?

'And then she looks at the fish, and she says, in a dreamy sort of way, "I wish – I wish – I wish that Malibongwe might win fame and recognition for his work."

'Bang! One wish done. Whoever Malibongwe might be then. She thinks again. "I wish, I wish, I wish – oh, I wish I could be cured of this awful virus."

'Silence. Then the fish says, in a rather small voice, "Dear woman, wishes only heal. They cannot cure."

'"OK," she says, in a small voice too. "I wish I could be healed."

'Bang! another wish gone down. She thinks again. "And – and – oh, our dear friend Toby Graaff –"'

Toby stiffened.

'Yes, you. She says, "Oh, I wish our dear friend Toby Graaff and his girlfriend will get together at last, for that is what I'd like for them, they've been so very kind."

'Bang! third wish done. Fish says, "Get a move on then,

good woman, let's make haste unto the beach." They get up and they go. And I find myself all weepy. A fuzzy feeling in my stone core. Some sense of purpose, some message to be given. And here you are and this is it – I'm meant to make your wish come true by telling you to get on with it, Toby Graaff. Stop acting dumb. You're a lucky guy.'

'Woah.'

'No, not woah. Just do it. And don't shoot the messenger. You intellectuals are far too shy. You live in the head. Or in sad repressed dreams. You don't see what I see. I see folk come and go. I see generations like the grasses and I see how the years flit past and then the silent grave. *Nox una perpetua dormienda*, as the poet said. *Carpe diem*, guy, get on with it. Fine to speak of marble tombs and enduring bronze and so forth, but the Taj Mahal's a cold and silent place and you've got a life to live and a wish to bring about, OK? Know what I mean?

'And one more thing – it's all very well you making fantasies about my sweet and girlish form – you see babes in the back of your head; but two can stereotype, I'll have you know. You gotta be a knight in shining armour like Sir Jasper de la Court. You gotta act. You gotta be a hero, score your babe, kiss away her tears and make it real.'

Toby nodded.

'And another thing. "Vanity of vanities, all is vanity, saith the Preacher." And this is true. But only if the heart is left out of the equation.'

The angel trembled with urgency to her wingtips. Her curly hair shook, her body swayed, as she pressed her point. 'Yes, we all come to the selfsame end. All the numbers add up to the same conclusion every time. There's nothing new under the sun. But there's all the difference in the heart, and since you have one, make use of it please.'

And then she gave a final twitch. She smoothed her mantle, she gestured once around her at the quiet graves, she assumed her timeless look of gentle sorrow, and her form grew very still.

The bee buzzed on; the dusty oleanders murmured secrets to the rising breeze; gnats floated in a cloud among the branches of the syringa tree; and Toby rose up from his gravestone. He knelt briefly, rose, and with new intent he turned his back upon that sad forsaken garden and those cooling antique stones.

KHAKI AND SCARLET

MALIBONGWE, FAR FROM HOME AND DEEP IN THOUGHT, sat beneath a kameeldoring bush at the side of a sandy track, miles from the nearest town. This was the tiny settlement of Pella, some ninety kilometres from Pofadder, in the most isolated, most arid region within the broad borders of the Republic.

'Which could it be?' he thought to himself. 'The valve timing or the ignition?' He hoped it was just a loose backplate on the ignition points. He fiddled at his battered offroad Yamaha, now coated in the fine red dust of the Northern Cape where this remote province followed on the fringes of the trackless Kalahari.

Malibongwe was exhausted – and not only by the heat and dust. He was commissioned by the great-grandchildren of a Canadian soldier who had died a century ago in the Anglo-Boer War, to find by means of divination the forlorn remains of their forefather. For hours he had struggled with the contending energies of various ancestors, *iminyanya* – his own, those of local Nama, Bushmen and Griquas, of long-gone Takhaar Boers, of Imperial Yeomanry, of Major McBurnie of Strathcona's Horse, late of Montreal in Lower Canada. '*Indaba*, my fathers,' he muttered weakly. Who would have thought this desert so thickly populated with the restless unseen?

He looked up as a rhythmic squeak and jingle came to his ears. It was his apprentice Anna Persens, the Subaltern. Riding in a cart with fat bald tyres, holding the reins to an ambling donkey, she jerked slowly closer to his bush.

'Well done,' he called. 'Now we can cart the bike to Pofadder for repairs.'

Anna, never one for words, flashed her dark eyes at the sauntering donkey's rear. A ten-mile journey had taken nearly an hour. She wondered what she was doing in this sandy waste. 'Fame and recognition' had she wished for Malibongwe? More like 'Lost in space'. Her chariot lurched off the track, dragging her through the thorny branches of Malibongwe's tree as the donkey made for the sparse and dusty leaves. She drank briefly from a flat round water bottle and tossed this vessel to her master.

'Hau!' cried the sangoma, 'where did you find this then, Anna?'

'A Bushman gave it to me.'

'Where did you meet this Bushman, Anna? Look at the back of the bottle, what do you see?' The steel surface was engraved with a regimental crest, and the initials A.E.M. – Albert Edward McBurnie, of course, the late Major McBurnie of Strathcona's Horse! 'And where did you fill it?'

'The Bushman filled it from a baobab tree.'

'Take me to your Bushman, if you please.'

So they heaved the Yamaha up into the little cart, and squatting awkwardly on the side, Anna teased the donkey into motion. Malibongwe paced beside her through the sand, fingering the weathered steel of the army-issue water bottle. His brow was furrowed. It seemed too easy, this chance find, this artefact whipped from nowhere, evidence from beyond.

A gravel road runs north from Pofadder to the old mission settlement of Pella. In the distance are the low-slung mountains which form the valley of the Orange River, the mighty Gariep. Some way up the road stands an isolated four-square whitewashed tin-roofed house. The interior is cool, bare but musty, an old man's home. At the back, among stunted lemon trees, Oom Servaas Vermaak appears to be executing a slow and curious ritual dance. With his battered broad-brimmed felt hat clamped as ever to that bony head, he swings and stands on one leg, then the other, waves his thin arms in delicate spirals. Two urchins in torn shorts peer through the plumbago hedge, eyes wide, stifling their laughter at the vision of Oom Servaas, 'Kwaai Servaas', vendor of vile liquor to the region's poor, miser, dedicated man of meanness and misery, now gyrating slowly beside his water tank between the scrubby trees. Only last week Oom Servaas was taken in by the new sergeant of police at Pofadder for practices best described as from the Old South Africa. Change came hard for him, if it came at all. Not a profound racist, he was just a bliksem, one who liked to take it out on others, especially the meek and humble, which meant the working folk of Pella district, the lightly built and light-voiced people known as Nama. What then is this tough old serpent doing?

As dusk tinged the sandstone with a golden glow and the dusty roads became kaleidoscopes of setting light, a donkey cart came into view, two weary comrades resting on the shafts, a battered old motorcycle in the back. Urchins and dogs raced wildly with the energy at sunset that only dogs and children muster, laughing and crying out, keeping easy pace with the shambling outfit.

'*Haai! Kyk die motorfiets*! A motorcycle! Vroom, vroom!' the urchins laughed and cheered. '*Kyk die ou toppie*, just look at the old guy! He's all covered in dust. They've been in the veld. Yay, yippee, faster, little donkey, faster!'

Anna tried to pretend they didn't exist. She brushed dust off her Out of Africa oatmeal pants and concentrated on the thought of a long cold Campari. Malibongwe's temper was less easy. He stood up on the shafts and shouted at the children.

'*Hambani, bafana. Kry julle weg, julle snot penkoppe!* Bugger off, you little pests!'

They responded with hoots of laughter and wilder leaps and gestures.

Then came a vision which made Anna stiffen and take note. Down the road towards them, drawing the little children to her like *muggies* to a glass of lemonade, a young woman with such perfect poise, such gentle sway of hips, such ease matched with purpose, such red hair and peachy skin as to make Anna bite her lip, in a burgundy crush skirt and close-cropped top, with a voice at once low and sweet, Kitty her name, Kitty Dippenaar, t'ai chi teacher at a New Age ashram which had risen on a plot outside the town. It was Kitty Dippenaar for whom old Servaas was gyrating in his *agterwerf*. It was Kitty whom the children clustered round as they left off taunting the morose donkey. It was this newcomer for whom Malibongwe's long face at last softened and broke into a spontaneous smile.

Anna shook the reins and twitched the donkey's rear with a switch of quince. They had yet to find their Bushman. No stopping to bandy with that over-decorated gypsy. Malibongwe'd better behave himself.

On and on they trundled, past the scrappy edgings of the town, on in the growing dusk, heading for a koppie in the middle distance from which a clutch of ancient baobabs rose up like tousled heads on thin bodies, black against the last glow of light.

A small man in khaki shorts and unbuttoned khaki shirt stood up among the tumbled stones. 'That's him,' said Anna. 'Hello, Dawid, here we are again. Can you tell this man – Malibongwe, he is called – where you found the water bottle?'

The small man cleared his throat. He had tight close hair, a light and almost oriental face, high cheekbones, and many wrinkles from many years of sun and dust.

'*Haai*,' he said, 'not an easy thing to say.'

Malibongwe sighed, stifling the urge to beat someone up, an urge not uncommon in the Northern Cape and largely due to vexations brought on by heat, thirst and distance. He took out his wallet and waved a fifty-rand note.

'*Haai*, sir, please. I do not mean that.' The Bushman bristled with dignity. 'I will explain.'

And so it turned out that the stainless steel water bottle was pilfered goods. Sidelong looks, gestures of innocence, wild conjecture onto half a dozen others, Saartjie, Maria, Kleinboy, Jantjie, Dwergie, Siena.

'No, my baas, I give it to the lady {*gesturing at Anna*} from my heart {*two-handed clasp at the thin bony breast*}. She is tired, she is *maar moeg*, she is *dors*. Jesus say, give it to the lady. I, Dawie Disselboom, I give her water. Living water, says the *Jirre*.'

'You did well,' Malibongwe interrupts. 'We aren't here to pick fights or blame anybody. All I want is to know where you found it. And it was good of you to rehydrate my apprentice. *Enkos'*. I thank you.'

So Dawie Disselboom led the weary pair another kilometre or two, and pointed out a foursquare old house which stood pale in the darkness, alone in the middle distance. Remote bright stars flared silver in the moonless night. On such a night as this, a century ago, the Canadians of Strathcona's Horse engaged in hot battle, bullets and bloodshed, with a Boer commando. Vibrations ran through Malibongwe's ears. He heard snatches of shouting, the crack and bark of Lee-Metford and of Mauser. He shook his head, and again it was the vexing donkey with its long ears silhouetted against the starlight, Anna muttering about cramp, and their wizened guide, who seemed reluctant to proceed farther down the track. Malibongwe gazed at the pale square house. The leaves of stunted lemon trees glimmered in the yard behind.

'Kwaai Servaas,' whispered Dawie Disselboom, and melted away into the night.

Meanwhile Kitty Dippenaar prepares the Pella mission hall for her weekly classes in t'ai chi and eurythmics. Chairs are stacked against the walls. On a schoolroom table she lays out bundles of sage and wild lavender, and lights a stick of incense.

'From the diaphragm,' she orders in her low sweet voice. 'In, and hold. Count of eight. And release. Can you feel your diaphragm, Chantelle?'

'Yes, Miss Kitty'.

'Slowly, slowly, Cornelius van Deventer. Here, let me hold.' The postmaster of Pella blushes as Kitty puts her arms about his thick midriff and presses on the solar plexus. Chantelle van Deventer's face reddens. If only Kitty were less fetching.

Kwaai Servaas practises diligently in the corner, unaware that he has visitors at home. The slightest word from Kitty, of approval or correction, is more therapy to his withered heart than all the reiki or past-life regression within her esoteric repertoire.

'Come, Servaas, you're doing well. Stretch into the space around you. Gently, Servaas, gently.' Servaas makes swimming movements in a bath of unaccustomed love.

Half a mile away, Malibongwe and Anna have their noses pressed against the panes of Kwaai Servaas's living room.

'I know it's here,' says the sangoma. '*Apha ekhaya apha.*'

'What?'

'I'm not sure, but it's hot. We're on track. Major McBurnie lies nearby, I feel it. We've got to get inside.'

Anna drew a skeleton key from her shoulder bag and fiddled with the lock.

The floor is part bare wood, part linoleum, worn and faded. In the moonlight emerge sad mementoes, the lineaments of frozen desire. A high dado with three items hanging: a faded framed photograph of a stern couple in churchgoing black; an unremarkable oil painting of a mountain pass; a certificate from the Agricultural Society. A set of souvenir teaspoons with municipal crests on them: Oudtshoorn and Lambert's Bay. The Voortrekker Monument and the Eeufees. Beside the passage door is a brassbound elephant's foot, and a tired blesbok trophy is screwed to the wall. A delicate shudder passes through Anna's modish frame. An oak sideboard, a decanter and a single glass under a clean cloth, marks of modest bachelorhood. Malibongwe steps quickly to the corner where an antique bandolier and a heavy Mauser rifle lie on a yellowwood kist. He raises them in his hands, and under the silvery moonlight he drinks the musty air.

'Ah. Aha! Vibrations, Anna, vibrations. Terrible, oh terrible, the smoke, the blood, the singing sword. McBurnie, Major McBurnie, Major, are you there?'

Deep silence, save for the ticking of the clock, and then: A-a-a-arooah! York-york-york, a-waaah! The donkey has gone randy. It bellows. It repeats this every minute for a quarter of an hour. During which time Servaas returns from t'ai chi practice, suffused with delight, for Kitty Dippenaar is coming in for a glass of hanepoot muscadel.

'*Wat die dooie donder!*' shouts Kwaai Servaas. 'Whose donkey is that pronking in my yard? So help me, I'll get the bliksems, they'll rue the day! Where's my gun?'

Kitty shook her head. 'Dear Servaas, so much anger.'

'Aa-aa-aa-arooah!'

'*Wat die donder maak julle mense in my werf? In my huis, sowaar!*'

'Hau! Anna, this is pandemonium. Hey, wait for me!' But Anna was halfway through the plumbago hedge, her long legs waving an inverted farewell to her master as he ran for the kitchen door.

'Arooh! York-york-york.'

'Stand still everyone! And shut up!' It was Kitty's voice. 'You too, you silly donkey.' She wore about her an unexpected mantle of authority, and Servaas and Malibongwe fell silent, shamefaced, unused to such exquisite power. Anna slithered from the hedge and joined the group. Over their shoulders the donkey's ears loomed in a large and silvery V, his long teeth bared for yet another convulsive but stifled cry.

The anger which spills from Servaas and scourges the lives of those who live in his neighbourhood runs deep in this withered old man. Like biltong, his goodness is all stored up and dried out. It will only be tasted when something softens. His goodness dried out some fifty years ago, or maybe even fifty-five, when his father took a strop to him; when his mother became like a washing-up lappie, either buried in grim tasks, silent in the concrete washbasin, or squeezed out on the line to dry, all the charm and colour blanched out, or stingingly used as a means of slapping him on his ears or about his bare legs.

Servaas had learnt to store away his goodness where it might never be seen – except for the advent of Marietjie, when he was seventeen and she was sixteen, and how Marietjie and he would sit for an hour together at sunset when the light was so golden and reflected in her hair, and would walk together in the veld to call the sheep, and would pick loquats; and how Marietjie's father, who was the dominee in Pofadder, said he would not have his daughter spending time with the son of such backveld people; and how he never got the courage to speak the words of his love. And this is now a poisoned well of stagnant waters.

All this Malibongwe discerns, for new vibrations have emerged from dado and mantelpiece, from kist and well-worn sofa, lapping up against him when the deadlocked group re-enter the house. Major McBurnie is forgotten. Kitty too feels something. Against her natural insouciance, so does Anna. She deftly mixes a powder from a twist of paper (something she thought she might try out on Malibongwe) into the tumbler of hanepoot muscadel.

This has an unexpected effect on Kwaai Servaas. He wipes his chin and glares at Malibongwe and Anna. He is going to deliver them a thousand words of wrath, but he swallows, chokes, turns red and gasps, 'Marietjie! *Sowaar, o, sowaar!* I buried her in the yard, not her I mean, I mean her ring. She sent it to me when she left for the Cape. *Ag, o sowaar, o die vrywende gekwaal van my gewetenis. O vergewe my, O God!* Oh me, oh my, the pain.'

Malibongwe has to dig deep. The sand of the yard slips back until he reaches the darker subsoil. Servaas has to dig deep.

Kitty sits beside him on the sofa, holding him round the shoulders. He sobs. He shudders. He looks small and frail, a forlorn remnant among the mementoes of a vanished universe. Anna digs deep to keep a measure of sympathy with both Kitty and Servaas, and a measure of patience with Malibongwe. She needs her sleep. She helps herself from the decanter and flips through old issues of *Farmer's Weekly*.

Finally it comes together. 'Marietjie!' cries Servaas, half rising from the sofa, the light of conversion suffusing his lined face. '*Ek het jou lief!*' 'Eureka!' cries Malibongwe as he struggles from his pit flourishing a rotted khaki helmet, a tarnished silver ring in his other hand. 'Yes!' cries Anna Persens, emerging from her *Farmer's Weekly*. 'Here's the man for me: "Wealthy well-groomed farmer seeks girlfriend for pleasure cruise. Send recent photo, SAE."'

Tumblers and tin mugs are fetched and toasts are drunk in hanepoot muscadel. Toasts to love, to courage, to Major McBurnie and to Servaas's father and his mother, to Marietjie wheresoever she might be. To the crippled shades, to ease them, to set them dancing in the silver moonlight all along the plumbago hedge and among the lemon trees where tiny buds of blossom refract the silver glow. T'ai chi for the living and the dead. There is the sound of hoofbeats down the dusty road; but not the beat of cavalry or commando. It is the hoofbeat of a sweet fat donkey mare, panting from the half-hour gallop in response to those convulsive cries. And from afar, from the koppie with its baobabs, sweet singing, light laughter and the clap of hands to naked dancing feet.

SHADES OF NIGHT

'YES, YES,' SAYS THE MINISTER IMPATIENTLY. 'These noises, you know, they emanate from certain quarters. Certain elements. And they – the media – they also make these noises. We don't listen to these things.'

Ozymandias (Ozzie) Brandvogel, freelance consultant, whispers in his ear.

'We will leave no stone unturned,' says the Minister, 'until the perpetrators have been brought to book.'

Ozymandias shakes his head. Wrong script. He whispers again.

'We have no comment,' says the Minister. 'All are deemed innocent until proven guilty in a court of law.'

The consultant comes forward. 'Thank you, Mr Ngingingini. We appreciate your time. You will hear from us in due course.'

'But – but –'

'*Thank* you. I'll show you out.'

'Looking into it. Structures in place. Thrash out the nitty-gritties,' says the Minister. 'Unpack your baggage. Legacy of . . .'

The door closes behind Ozzie, and Malibongwe is back in the antechamber where the secretary points to his green trilby and his coat and returns to her computer screen.

'*Hayi*,' mutters Malibongwe. 'It's no good.'

His friend the District Nurse sits down, dispirited, on the wooden bench in the lobby. Who else to try? What avenue? A security guard hovers, and Babalwa and Malibongwe leave the Ministry for a cup of coffee at the Wimpy around the corner.

'Can't get through the officialdom,' says Malibongwe. 'That consultant has him in his power. Same story all over.'

'The one called Brandvogel? He's *bad*. They're all bad but he's the worst. They call it outsourcing. It's just a gravy train – at least fifty per cent of the budget goes down the throats of these consultants.'

'Ja. And how they get contracted is another thing. *Baantjies vir boeties*. Kith and kin. One hand washing the other. Two heads in the same cap.'

Malibongwe had written half a dozen times for this appointment with the Minister of Progress in the Provincial Government of the Eastern Cape, Mpuma Koloni. They'd tossed him a bone, given him five minutes, and the door had closed again. Ozymandias Brandvogel. Consultant. The new face of governance, like bees at the honeypot.

Malibongwe was in Bisho, the administrative capital of the Eastern Province, with a long petition signed by many of his people, amaXhosa, who lived now in shanties in the ranging shacklands on the broad and sandy wastes of the Cape Flats. They were folk who came to Cape Town for a better life than what was theirs back home in the ancestral rural areas, among the eastern hills and woods – but this was not the simplest answer to their plight. The petition called for better infrastructure in the rural places, clinics, service delivery, decent sanitation, schoolbooks in isiXhosa, and the prompt supply of anti-retrovirals for the ill. So much – there was so much. He slumped under the burden of the weight of history, the dull weight of neglect, the urgent weight of people's need. *He* was dulled. He was thwarted and beaten. Who shall see to this? Unto whom to turn?

The titihoya calls forlorn on tough-grassed hillsides. Over the brow of the great hill, from the crowns of thorn trees, come the hadeda in ragged flight, one, two, three. Red and orange aloe flowers light the grey-green landscape like clustered torches. The aloes march up the hillside row on row, the army of the Gideonites. The tongues of flame on talking souls.

Malinbongwe takes a branch of aloe in his hand, bright torch. Alert, bareheaded, unshod, he walks up the Hill of Dreams. Behind him lies the valley and the smaller hillsides, the foothills of the Amatola Mountains, with their dotted houses, kraals, the broad land of goat and cow. The sparkling tin on water cisterns or roofs.

The sun is strong but low. Stare at it, and the sky darkens with indigo, and the sight blackens.

Malibongwe stands alone on the broad hilltop. The world is silent. Not a bird is singing. There is a murmur from the wind, but nothing else. And the wind too now drops. The sunlight whitens on the great stone. All colour is leached from the grass, the sky, the earth. It is neither white nor black. It is the silent glaze of sunlight at the threshold.

From the blue sky comes a thunderclap, the bolt of lightning. *Umqhekrezo wombane*, the true firebird of divination.

Malibongwe's hand is singed. In the blackened hand he holds the aloe flower. His sight has gone. His lungs burn. He is limping. Either he has twisted his ankle on the climb to the hilltop or the firebird's bolt has paralysed his leg. He stoops and enters the bright dark.

Down through layers where the worms grittily work, through koffieklip and wet limestone, through sedimented records of the upper world, he goes. There are bullet shells, coins – George III shillings, Victorian pennies – few, but they are there. Pebbles, flints, stone and horn and bone, the bones of cattle, of men and women. Then the rock, and fossil reptiles, birds, ferns, and tiny crustaceans. Malibongwe's mouth and nose are filled with grit. The dark embeds him. His keen ears pick up the sound of mineral growth, the slow expansion through the matrix, the creep of bloom of manganese and red iron in the stone, the tinkle of crystalline felspar and agate. The everpresent drip of lime-laden water, the trickle, the prickling growth of stalagmite.

Here is where the world of trees and animals and men and women first arose – and whence they will rise again. *Uhlanga*, the navel of the world, omphalos, deep source.

'Hau! 'Tis young Malibongwe!' came a gruff voice in the dark.

'The son of S'bo?'

'That's the one. S'bo, son of Matata – what became of S'bo now?'

'Went to the mines, *ndoda*. Never came back.'

'Ai. That gold earth. Wouldn't want to dwell down there.'

'You squeamish, old man?'

'*Hayi*. Don't be a fool. How can we talk with all that digging? Explosives? Greed?'

'You like it here?'

'You! You youngsters! What better soil than ours?'

Malibongwe stood quietly, waiting for the shades to settle. The ancestors, *iminyanya*. How the generations wrangled!

'Never mind about the mines. Malibongwe now – he's the one who left the cattle, who went to school with the *mlungu*?'

'*Ewe*. He was bright. *Bright*. He won a scholarship to the great school in iRhini. Grahamstown. Hee hee. Learning Latin and isiNgesi. English. We watched him carefully. You should have seen him doing cricket now! Paf! He ran and cast the ball so fast. And whack! He stood and hit the ball with the wooden bat. Bang! He was going to be *ugqirha*, doctor, the modern doctor.'

'What happened then?'

'It was still the days of apartheid. He had to get permission to go to the great school. He had to get permission to go to university. There were the uprisings in the 1980s. Ai, those were bad times. So much evil, and so much death.'

'I remember, uncle. The land was under *ukuthwasa*. Birth pains and much sacrifice.'

'I am speaking.'

'Was he with the boys to the mountain? Did he do *umrhabulo* – initiation?'

'All was done as it should be done. But as I was going to say, the days of trouble – the state of emergency – it was his brother, Malibongwe's brother – that's how it happened. It was the thing we try not to speak about. Ai, the thing that was done to him.'

Malibongwe knew what was to come – the telling of the story of the death of Lulama – a story he had taken years to settle in his soul. Lulama was his older brother and a teacher at a village school. Lulama was mistaken as an *impimpi*, an informer for the police's special branch under that old and awful dispensation. What was done, in those mad days, to informers was the necklace. The car tyre around the neck, the petrol, the scramble for the matches, the shouting crowd, the kicks and blows as the fuel went up, the stink of rubber, the blaze, the horror, *the pain*. The scattering crowd and the dying man left on the ground. Unhallowed ground. Scorched inhuman earth.

'I have spoken.'

'Ai, ai, you've spoken, old man. It is bitter.'

'And this is how Malibongwe came to *ukuthwasa*. He was there when it happened and he watched and he could do nothing. And he fell ill, fell into *ukuthwasa*. Gave up the university. He was called by the great Mzimkhulu to be his pupil. He was sick. So sick! He couldn't eat. He couldn't sleep. He walked like a man in a bad dream. But slowly, slowly, Mzimkhulu brought him back to life. Mzi. *He* was a man!'

Malibongwe listened to the old ones as if to another life.

He had indeed been born again, gently, sometimes roughly, under the guidance of great Mzi. His mission now was to make things right – *ukulungisa*. No more should people suffer as his brother suffered, as the others suffered so to make them do such things.

But – but oh, the anguish at the thought of what is now, these latter days so long removed from that time of hope and newness for the nation back in 1994. The time-serving Minister of Progress and his predatory mentor, Brandvogel – and it seems as though these rulers have journeyed very far from the people who still go hungry, who live off tiny pensions, who trudge for hours to hospitals and clinics where there are more vacant posts than nursing staff. And how the children run wild, for the schools are ill-appointed and the syllabus is incomprehensible and the textbooks all in English. And the evil spirit of the epidemic has its grip upon the land, the HIV and AIDS. And the young men and women go by bus to Cape Town, where they live in growing acres of tin and cardboard shanties because they are too many there, and there is no work and all the promise of the city is a dream, but meanwhile the green hills are empty and the fields in disarray.

The deep dark earth was breathing. Out of the gloam – *isithoko-thoko* – and through those muffled voices came the great Mzi. Forward, stepping firmly, wordless, with grave salutation to Malibongwe came Mzi. He stood and looked in silence at the younger man. His eyes were deeply socketed, his mouth pursed tight in earnest. Without speech he grasped Malibongwe's arm and pointed.

On, with Mzi as his guide, with the aloe as his torch, Malibongwe trod towards the circles of the shades. Between these galleries of the shades and Malibongwe and his guide there flowed a great river, dark and broad and strong. Here were the river people, the merfolk, the ones who summoned and gave answers, the demanding ones, the knowing ones, some teasers, some teachers, the spirits of the water.

Beyond this dark flood the great galleries came into view, and there were crowds of people, so many, one would not have thought the harvest was so rich – gibbering shades, their mouths open and their arms outstretched, men, women and children, the people of the red blanket, of the soil, of the land: amaGcaleka, and abaTembu, and amaPedi, and amamPondo, and the amaFingo somewhat abashed and at the rear, and amaRharhabe of the Amatola, and amaNdlambe named from their chieftain's ox, and the many nations. Like the rustle of a thousand thousand leaves in autumn, so the countless numbers with their olapodrida of tongues, their swaying jostling murmur in the dark.

Great stern-faced Hintsa and Sandile and Makana and Ngqika or Gaika, Maqoma and Ndlambe the warrior with the feathers of the blue crane on his head, the chiefs, iziNkosi, arms folded, heads held high, clad in leopard skins and the beads and feathers of their rank. And highest among them the old chief Phalo, head of the paramount house. And behind him, distant, wreathed in shining dark and even older, the founder of the great house of all of amaXhosa, fabled Tshiwo himself. Malibongwe cast his eyes down before them with the fullest measure of respect that threatened to burst his beating heart.

Mzi bade Malibongwe halt. From the river rose a merman hairy in his aspect and all clotted with the river snail and weeds. This wild and unkempt thing went plunging to the farther side, and there a modest shade was waiting – and was borne back to the master and his pupil on the shoulders of the river man: Lulama! Could it be? His late brother Lulama!

Malibongwe turned in excitation to Mzi, who drew Lulama near and stood back from the pair.

'Lulama! My brother! *Kunjani wena?*' The emptiness of words at such a moment did not stay Malibongwe's urgent address. 'O my brother! Lulama! How are you? What have you to say to me? Ah, do speak!'

And Lulama smiled at Malibongwe and he spoke. '*Ndiyaphila, ubhuti wam.* I am well. *Ndiphilile kakuhle.* It is good to see you. There is much to talk of. It is given that I may speak with you. Do not attempt to take me in embrace, however.'

As he spoke, so a tongue of flame rose up and brightened on his head.

Malibongwe longed to hug his brother, to take his hand, to fall upon his neck and hold him arm-in-arm as they used to when carefree in the village of their youth. Instead he stood and stared with eager eyes and open mouth at the familiar form.

'And our tata and our mama are both well – for they are with me here.'

'Yes? O tell me more of all our people – but first of your own purpose and your state.'

'What took place was then, my brother. It was an error of the people, and they know it now. They cannot speak of it from their distress. And look upon me – there are no signs of hurt upon my person. I crossed this dark river and I was restored, for that is how it works.'

Lulama continued: 'And you are come to me that I may speak of further restoration. We know the pity in the land, for daily more shades come to us and tell of brevity of life, tell of the illness in Mzantsi Afrika, tell of poverty and trouble and the violence in the land. Yes, you have been unto the courts and offices of the politicians, this I know. You have argued for the plight of all *abantu.* You have sought to make things better for the people.

'Know this, my brother. All must come here in their time. And what is time, the time of the elephant or the mouse, the ancient cycad or the season's grass? What is the time of man or woman? All cross over to that yonder shore and all will come to pass when it is meant; by which I mean a rising up in newness and in strength.

'Yes, a rising up to newness of life among the men and women, and the cattle too. Yes, the very vision that the prophetess once had, Nongqawuse the prophetess and her prophets; but she confused it with wrong timing – for the timing is not known nor ever will be in the minds of men.

'You, Malibongwe, you are called to heal, to make good. Many have this calling, each in their own way. Know that you can only do your best within your sphere. Know that there is newness in every moment, every action, every thing. Know that *ukuthwasa* is our true state – the calling through pain and trouble into newness every day.

'You, Malibongwe, must return to the upper air, return and leave this grave and placid place of waiting. It is not for you to see the future chiefs, the South Africa – the Africa – that is yet to be. It is not for you to see the Presidents, Kings, and *iziNkosi* yet to come, or Peoples yet to farm our soils and tend our flocks and herds. Know but this, that all come here – black and white – and all are one, and all shall be again. Sown in weakness, raised in strength, O my brother. Know but this, that you shall work for newness and joy and goodness in the upper world, where laughter always heals, where hearts are eased and reconciliation then takes place.

'Leave your greater cares and tend the lesser. Go about your tasks among the mixed nations of Ntshona Koloni, the black and white and all the races, and all the paths of faith. Sow seeds of laughter and joy and set the minds at ease, and other things will follow. Let there be no hidden evil in men's hearts. I, Lulama, have now spoken.'

The tongue of flame upon his brother's head now dwindled and Lulama gently smiled and turned away his face.

'But – but stay, my brother!'

Mzi shook his head and ushered Lulama back to the bank of the great river, and the hairy merman rose again and bore him to the farther side.

Mzi again led Malibongwe on. The younger man was all in much amaze, for the joy of meeting Lulama, for the bitter joy of such brief converse, and for the import of his brother's words. To his heart he took those words, and vowed he would be guided by them. *Kancinci-kancinci* – little by little – with modesty and good humour in his breast, so would he play his part in healing of the people.

And on they moved, and unto other galleries, to Mali-bongwe's surprise: the sheepskin-wearing Khoekhoen with their ancient tongue, and their kapteins and their descendants who spoke in Cape Dutch and Afrikaans; and in earnest knots the black-clad missonaries who had taken them under their bright-lit wing; and lo! amaNgesi and amaBhulu – grim-faced English settlers, rough Boer farmers – these too had planted and reaped and gone to ground below this fertile soil. Malibongwe looked towards the great Mzi, who still spoke naught but nodded sombrely and trod on. Malibongwe moved with him, glancing back at the settler shades in wonder. They too had their dwelling in this earth! Though true enough their galleries were shallow and the waters of the dark stream lapped up at them with seeming challenge.

Thus did Malibongwe pass before this great cloud of witness, community of saints and sinners, the circles of the ancestors, the ones who've gone ahead.

And then there came a gust of fresh air, and a faintest light in front. With whirring of wings there darted a small bird. It circled Malibongwe. Mzi turned to him, nodded silently, and was gone.

The bird darted forward and came back and seemed to want to lead him. He followed it. He followed it through narrow shafts where the waters of the river tossed and foamed and roared. The light grew brighter, the air more lively. He found himself skirting a great whirlpool, a roaring maelstrom, where the river plunged and sank into the deeper depths. His head reeled at the thunderous display, and shrinking to the wet walls he made his careful way beside the seething abyss.

And then, accompanied by the trickle of a bright spring, sole vestige of the waters of the underworld, he was out in the upper air, among the aloes and acacia thorns, the sky now rich and redolent with rain. The bird, the rainbird, soared up and to the paunchy clouds, and Malibongwe sank down to rest at the cave's protective mouth. Too exhausted to note the faint paintings in the cave, images of the water people, of the bird, of eland and of elephant, he lay and fell asleep for many hours.

Malibongwe woke as from a dream. The land was crystal clear and fresh from rain. He sat up and stretched, and started on his recollection of the visions that had passed. Lulama! And great Mzimkhulu! And the countless peoples – Malibongwe had been called to something rare and strange, *indaba* with the shades themselves.

As he made his way down the hillside he rejoiced and gave praise in his heart. *Kancinci-kancinci* – little by little – he would do as Lulama advised. He would use his talents such as they were in ways that made a difference in his sphere. He felt a burden lifted from him and he felt a laughter; not the foolish laughter of the crackle of the thorns in fire, but the laughter of deep welling springs – a laughter that meant to work through all his flesh and spirit and to give him strength and love. Birds above swooped and dallied in the fragrant air and Malibongwe raised his arms and sang out praise as down he came to fields and huts.

He passed the fields, the musing cattle and the grazing goats, the women at their tasks, the kraal, the reservoir, and trading store. There he found his motorcycle and packed his things and set off to the highway. Calling to the people in the fields, he rode with love and joy. Trust in each to be their selves. Never mind the sad corruption at the top – Brandvogel and his kind will always be with us – trust in themselves to make a difference. He waved at the umfaans who sat huddled against the winter breeze, in their upturned wheelbarrows like little turtles in their shells along the road, waiting for the sacks of mealie meal. They waved back and grinned and called out words that mingled with the wind.

His scorched hand was the hand he waved. Babalwa back in Bisho would tend it for him, and then he must go on, back to Cape Town, to his work. Back, he thought with kind amusement, back to the many petty madnesses of town.

RED BULL

Malibongwe meant to break his journey home, to spend an hour or two with an old friend at the University of Fort Hare, in the tiny town called Alice, eDikeni in his mother tongue, at the foot of the Amatola Mountains. In these mountains hangs the upland region called the Hogsback, a lush elfin world of giant fern and cycad, hardwood and shining waterfall, poised above the winding pass that runs down into Alice at its foot.

Malibongwe enjoyed the mountain pass as he leant into the tight curves on his Yamaha. The big barking single cylinder responded to the cooler mountain air and he plied the torque, practising his skill along the kloofs. The trick is always just to watch the road ahead, its curve, its camber, its serpent coils; never to focus on the other vehicles, or the roaming cattle. Use your lateral vision for those and for the view, but focus mainly on the coiling road, and like a sure cable it will draw you where you ought to go.

Young men stood at the side of the road with clay animals for sale to passing tourists – hogs, for the Hogsback, and Nguni cattle, pinched out in red clay and painted with fanciful white markings. Malibongwe didn't want one. He knew that the clay was only sun-dried and would break up in his haversack. He did stop, though, to buy a prickly pear or two from the blanketed young women who were vending these from buckets at the roadside. He took them in his gloved hand and put them gingerly into his bag – the fine hairlike spines were vicious.

So was the nail he rode over as he entered Alice. His rear tyre sighed and flattened and the Yamaha snaked its way perilously into town between the lively dogs and ruminating goats. There's no town like Alice – while it hosts a venerable university, it barely merits municipal status. Picturesque but crumbling nineteen-twenties bungalows hidden behind huge unkempt figs and willows, a rambling hotel (the Prickly Pear) and off-sales with more holes than doors, the usual broad and informal supermarket cum farmers' co-op, a two-pump petrol station, and little else. No chance of getting a new inner tube in Alice. He'd have to overnight and phone for one from Grahamstown.

He sighed and shrugged. Travellers learn patience. One thing at a time. First, let's go and say hello to Valiant. He'll put me up for the night at any rate, and we've got lots to talk about. Mandeville College, for instance.

Dr Valiant Kholwane was an old 'varsity friend of Malibongwe's. He was now a senior lecturer in the University of Fort Hare, and waiting to hear about promotion to professor. Mandeville was Valiant's old Oxford college and Malibongwe was headed there in a month's time, to give a paper at ICSATH, the International Conference of Shamans and Traditional Healers.

Malibongwe traded jests with the security guards and entered the campus of Fort Hare. He found his way to the Arts Block and to the Faculty of Humanities. He went door by door until he saw the tag with Valiant's name. He knocked. He heard a scuffling from within. He listened, waited, knocked again. More scuffling and a muffled curse.

'Valiant? *Mhlobo wam!* It's me, Malibongwe! Are you there?'

The door burst open and the large form of Valiant stood there sweating, his tie undone, his collar unbuttoned, his hair awry.

'*Hayi!* Malibongwe! *Molo, mhlobo!* How are you? What a surprise! Er – come in, come in.'

Malibongwe stepped into the office and stared in astonishment. The room looked as though a tornado had struck. The windows were smashed, the phone hung from the electric light, the floor was a sea of papers. Books had been flung all over, and Valiant's computer seemed to have a most alarming screensaver, a fireball that pulsed and sent out smoke.

Valiant grabbed his briefcase, locked the door against the awful scene, and shuffled his great bulk hastily from the building. Malibongwe pushed his motorcycle alongside the troubled scholar, and they made their way to Valiant's house in the pot-holed main street. Frangipani, fig, tacoma and poinsettia, a pleasant garden, nice twenties woodwork, a solid house, and filled with books and native carvings. Valiant was as yet a bachelor – he had deep difficulties with his inner life – a kind and loving man but more suited to modernity than the customs of his clan. Great-grandmother Gogo Noqongqothwane insisted on the ancient ways but Valiant had no taste for an arranged marriage and the payment of lobola cattle and a partner who'd be no more than a bearer of his children.

Valiant's life thus far was dedicated to his scholarship. His doctoral thesis which he'd defended at Oxford was on the intellectual resistance and engagement of black men of letters in South Africa in the later nineteenth century. Tiyo Soga, John Knox Bokwe, John Langalibalele Dube and their peers. This was about their own struggle with modernity and colonial attitudes and old customs and new faith. Valiant was a part-time preacher in the African Methodist Episcopalian Church, admirer of the progressive reasoning of Protestantism, a man for whom *Pilgrim's Progress* (*Uhambo Lomhambi*) was an enduring allegory of light and reason, soul and mind. 'Behold, I make all things new', the declaration of his Saviour, was embroidered by a student and hung above his mantelpiece.

Malibongwe knew and respected Valiant's views. The scholar held Malibongwe in esteem for his own tough role as broker between the old and new. They switched on the kettle and the toaster.

'Valiant, have you got something I can put on my hand?'

'What happened to it?'

'A long story, old man. I went up the Hill of Dreams.'

'The Hill? Thaban' iPhupha?'

'Mm.'

'I see.' Valiant looked carefully at Malibongwe. 'Few go there nowadays. It's only the elders, like old Gogo Noqongqothwane.'

'Gogo? How is she?'

'Shoo. She's a hundred now. No identity papers to prove it but they've been keeping tally for the past thirty years, and it seems to be the case.'

Valiant chuckled as he got out a bottle of Glenfiddich from the cabinet and poured two tots.

'Here's to your health, my healer friend! Here, put some Zam-Buk on your hand.'

'And to your health, Valiant. Longlive. And your promotion. Any word about it?'

Valiant frowned. But before he could reply, there came yelling and wild singing upon the rising wind. There was the sound of smashing glass, and shouting. Gunshots. Screams.

'The Friday night mob in the Prickly Pear down the road. It's like that every week.'

A car revved and screeched its tyres. Hooting, and the sound of banging on metal. Heavy metal music too, more gunshots muffled by the drums.

Malibongwe clucked in sympathy. He knew small towns well. On Saturday mornings there'd be no sign of havoc. The torn-off bumpers and wheel hubs would be gone, the bodies carted off, the broken glass swept up, and only the new holes in hotel walls would speak of Friday leisure. In a society in transition, folks took their Friday leisure seriously.

This time it sounded as though there was something else. A crowd came running down the street, a crowd united in its purpose of hasty flight. And the police van was with them, not in pursuit as in the days of struggle against apartheid, but fleeing too. Malibongwe and Valiant peered through the curtains.

'Goodness. What is going on?'

'I wish I could get a post somewhere else,' said Valiant, 'but as you know there's little going in the humanities these days. Lucky enough to be getting promotion here. If it comes off, alas.'

'Oh? I thought it was in the bag.'

'Ha. So did I. But things have happened, like what you saw in my office this afternoon.'

'Tell me more.'

Valiant meant to speak, but there came a bloodcurdling cry, an explosion, and the hotel burst into flames.

'These tsotsis go too far! I'm calling the flying squad in Grahamstown. And the fire department in Fort Beaufort. They could be here in half an hour.'

Malibongwe heard despair beneath the urgency in Valiant's voice as the scholar fumbled with the phone. Malibongwe was alert now, sensing something beyond the normal scale of mayhem. He went to look outside.

He opened the door and saw the hotel in flames against the inky night. A dreadful sight as always, the familiar changed by fire, the windows breathing flame, the roofline rocking in the firestorm, the dark made wild and darker yet by shooting sparks.

'Dear God, I hope nobody's trapped inside!'

And then he saw – he saw a human form, a giant of a man taller than the doorframe, a dark thing with fire blazing from its eyes, and brandishing a machete or a sword. In the other hand it held a long and smoking revolver. It stood within the open doors and breathed out fire as it gestured and capered. And a wild-haired doxy hung around its neck, she too with fire in her eyes and hair, and spuming bottle in her hand. Malibongwe shut his eyes and turned away. Can it be? Please not. He feared the worst.

Someone poked him in the kidney. He opened his eyes, looked down and saw, standing on Valiant's threshold, the shortest oldest woman he had ever seen. Barely as high as Malibongwe's elbow, withered into herself, shrunken. She gathered her mantle about her in a queenly fashion, and her withered face peeked out above the folds. She stood, she raised her withered arm, and pointed with her finger at the cowering figure of Dr Kholwane. 'EEEE,' she released a long breath at him. 'EEEeee. Ayiiiii.'

'Gogo!' stammered Valiant Kholwane putting down the telephone. '*Kunjani wena?*'

'*Hayi!* Don't play nice with me, *umntwana!* EEE-I-I-I-I-I!' The crone ululated in the doorway for a while.

'P-please come in, Gogo,' stuttered Valiant. 'It's mad and dangerous outside. What can I do for Gogo?'

'AAAyI-I-I-I-I! *Hayikona, bhuti!* I speak here where I stand. Now listen!'

She held her hands over her ears and ululated for another thirty seconds, as if gauging resonances on the inner ear.

'She – she's going into a trance,' Valiant muttered to Malibongwe. 'I hope she's got her epilepsy medicine with her.'

Still keeping her hands cupped over her ears, she rolled her eyes back as far as they would go. The mantle fell from her thin body and she stood in a pitiful thin cotton smock, with a handsome rope of beads about her tiny neck.

'He's here, he's back, he's come to claim his own, he wants to drive us out, he'll stand and fight until the clans are dead and driven to the wind; the ancestors are angry that he roams our land and they are rising up in arms to fight. Blood and fire, wind and water overwhelm the land. EEEE-I-I-I-I-I-I-I!'

'Gogo? Malibongwe, pass her the carafe please. I think she's dehydrated again. Dehydration brings this on. I wish she'd at least take water when she goes on her monthly fasts.'

Malibongwe gestured to Valiant to stay silent. 'Mother,' he addressed the crone. 'Mother, do you mean – do you mean *him*?'

'*Ewe!* Yeeessss, oh yes, he's back! And all because of the likes of you, you unbelievers, modernisers, coconuts, collaborating milk chocolates, you who tamper with the ways of amaNgesi, you who've wandered from the olden paths, you who do not sacrifice, who walk with dogs, you who – you who . . .'

'See?' hissed Valiant as he hunkered down behind his couch. 'See what I mean? I don't know what to do. Trying to build a career and this is what I get. She haunts me even on the campus and the committee's taking notice. How do you think my office got trashed today? Go on, what do you think, Malibongwe? She did it – she went and stuck pins into my door or something.'

'No,' muttered Malibongwe. 'I don't think so. No, you're fine. You're on the right path, absolutely. *Indlela ye' nkolo.* It's something else, and it's not going to be easy. I'm afraid it's – I've just seen him in the Prickly Pear – it's *Black Jim!*'

Blonde Clementina stretched, yawned, and smiled. 'It's like being in fairyland,' she whispered, running her hand down Toby's spine. He rolled over and kissed her. Outside, the early dawn was teased by tinkling rain-frogs and by clucking guinea fowl, and the francolin and cooing dove. Mist lifted in the early rays, and dewdrops magnified the spider and the beetle and mantis as they stirred on their leaves and beds of grass. The Hogsback is a prime place for tourists and for lovers. The mountain air, the virgin springs, the woods and highland meadows tell of that Garden where First Man and Woman walked in grace. Where First Beasts walked beside them, and they discoursed all together as they gently grazed and plucked the fairest fruits.

Their host, a shaven-headed Western Buddhist, tapped on the door with fresh-baked bread and pawpaws. On the tray, with a frangipani flower, was a complimentary gift, one of the little red clay oxen that the local children make for sale to tourists.

'Meditation in half an hour,' the Buddhist whispered. 'And the mystic maze is best walked between the hours of eight and nine. Your robes are in the closet.'

Toby chuckled. 'Meditation. I'd sooner gaze at *your* navel, darling,' he declared to Clementina, and when the door was closed they renewed their recently engaged embrace.

Was it Horace or Catullus who had written poems about the sweet campaigns and combat of the love bed? Toby's intrusive mind shifted to the image of other battles, bloody and protracted fighting in these very woods and kloofs, when the Amatola was the site of desperate engagement between the amaXhosa and the British. How things have turned round! Peace poles, prayer wheels and mazes, bed-and-breakfast for gentle guests in gracious country homes.

Clementina pummelled him back to focus. 'Hey! What about *me*?'

'Sorry, sweetheart.'

'Ooh, aah, that's better. Lots of catching up to do, darling. What got you going after all this time?'

'It was the fish that did it.' But his words were lost in mortal combat.

High on the Hogsback above the winding pass, out of time and unseen by Clementina and Toby and by their gentle hosts, there marched the shades of amaXhosa with their spears borne up like spines of prickly pear, like bristles on a wild pig's back. And towards them marched the redcoat regiments, ragged, broken-booted, led by amaMfengu and the Khoekhoe scouts, their muskets and Martini-Henrys on their shoulders. Thick undergrowth and river-courses held them, but still the forces neared. Drums beat, the side drum of the redcoats, the cowhide of the Xhosa. Horses whinnied and fat gamebirds fled their coverts. Leopard and gazelle made good their distance while vultures hovered overhead.

The forces closed, 'mid shouts, alarum, bugle and the war cry of the clans. Bull and bulldog met and fought. And red blood was shed among the thorns and vines and stones; and both sides bled; and Ngqika fell, and Maqoma, and Sandile, and went down chief among the ancestors; and after nine long and bloody wars this land of amaXhosa fell to the pale foe.

At eight that morning Malibongwe went to Valiant's phone to order an inner tube for his Yamaha, but the old black bakelite began to ring before he dialled. Valiant picked it up.

'Dean Swift? Yes, sir, I'm fine. Thank you. What? My word! The library! I'll be there now.'

He turned, ashen, to Malibongwe. 'Someone – or something – in the library – trashing it! Security's not coping. The dean's called the police but I live closest. Got to go and see what's happening.'

The two of them dashed down the street.

'Your Black Jim's rampaged in the Knowledge Commons! The students' internet! Proverbial bull in the – er – ah – he's tossing books out of the windows, he's heading for the archives, they said,' puffed Valiant. 'He's got a box of matches!'

Fort Hare has long roots in association with the venerable old mission school of Lovedale College, and has been the alma mater of generations of black intellectuals. Its collections were irreplaceable testimony to the rise of a modern African intelligentsia. Valiant and Malibongwe both knew what lay at stake.

'Poltroons! Cowards! Jackanapes! Sweepings! Call yourselves troopers, you craven curs? Set to! Charge! Fire and steel! Put 'em to the sword!'

The ghastly voice, mad clarion, echoed round the quad. 'Burn, you blaggards, burn! I hate learning! I hate books! I hate Dr Arnold and I hate – er – Rugby. The school, I mean. I hate reading! I hate writing! Burn, you rags and chapbooks, burn!'

Black Jim, colonel of dragoons, was on campaign; they could see him up on the second floor through the high library windows. And who was his mistress? Who was that alarming dark-eyed one with the flaming hair that rampaged at his side? From her fingers crackled sparks, while he skewered books upon his sabre.

'And as for you 'varsity lot,' he cried, 'who wants to be an inkhorn swot? I could've got into Oxford if I wanted, but I didn't want, so there! And I hate it when my enemy, which is these amaXhosa, think they're uppity-smart and get mission-trained and read and write, damned treason ain't it then, and *so* much, and *there*, and *there* again, for all your slavish books and learning!'

Colonel Jim swung and cut with his sabre, and then turned to fumbling with the box of matches while his woman leant against him.

Malibongwe feared a second, more destructive, conflagration. He showed himself to the dread spectre and let loose a stream of taunts: 'Ya, fat fag, bellhop, bottom of the class, only got your commission because your tata bought you one, didn't you? Ya, you wouldn't know your drill from your dance card would you, poncy Pom!'

Black Jim peered down into the quad from his high window. 'You! You again! Meet your end, you swarthy fiend!'

His form vanished from the long casement and Malibongwe guessed his ruse had worked: Jim was coming down to meet him. But what next? How to face this demon hand-to-hand?

A battered truck drew up. There was Gogo Noqongqothwane, sitting in front beside the driver. Gogo had a scowl of fierce intent and in her hand a butcher's cleaver. On the back of the old Dodge there snorted a great Nguni bull.

Gogo alighted from the truck just as Jim appeared at the library door. Their eyes met across the quad in mutual understanding. He waved his sabre and she waved her cleaver back.

'*Now* I show how we fight amaNgesi!' cried Gogo, making as if to dart across the quad and tackle him. But it was a little war dance rather than attack. She tottered and toyi-toyied, brandishing her cleaver. Then she signalled to the driver to release the bull from the truck.

'Sacrifice, sacrifice, blood and guts,' she cried. 'This is how we do it here!'

Black Jim cowered for a precious second, then he left the protection of the doorway. The doxy came behind him, and he advanced with little skirting and defensive movements, swinging out with his sabre, bright eyes watching every move that Gogo made.

Gogo stood back and twitched and cackled while the truck driver manhandled the great bull. Moaning, fretting, sweating, Valiant watched from behind Malibongwe. The mistress in her long skirts, the sweeping steps made by Black Jim, the bull, the colonnaded quad, it might have been a passage from an Andalusian paso doble or a Sevillana.

Gogo prodded the bull to make it bellow, and her cleaver was about to slice the great beast's under-neck when two tourists wandered in and the blonde one yelled with piercing voice, '*Stop!* Stop I say! Old woman, leave that bull alone!'

'Toby! Clementina! Get back! Whatever are you doing here?' Malibongwe hissed at them in surprise; but there was Clementina wrestling the cleaver from Gogo's hand. She grasped Gogo by the scruff of her thin smock and blazed a blue-eyed challenge at the scene.

'We – er – this *is* a surprise,' said Toby, taking stock. Black Jim was on the move again, circling warily towards both Gogo and Malibongwe.

'What's that in your hand?' Malibongwe hissed at Toby. 'Give it here. Quickly, please.'

Toby held out his toy clay ox.

'Give me that, Toby. Quickly! *Nkos'!* Anybody got a pocket knife?'

Toby took out his Swiss army knife. But Gogo screeched, '*Hayi!* No! Not that *umlungu*'s foreign blade! This big coconut must do the thing!' She pointed, quivering, in Valiant's direction.

Malibongwe took the souvenir and put it on the ground. 'You must do this, Valiant. I'm sorry. Just do it please. Just stomp on it.'

Valiant demurred. He dug in his heels. 'No! – one Sacrifice sufficeth and one only, for all of time,' gasped the scholar. Their adversary saw him hesitate and made a dash at them.

'All right,' said Malibongwe grimly. 'So be it. Get back, Valiant, here comes Black Jim!'

As Malibongwe pushed him in the chest, he kicked the clay toy behind the weighty man. Valiant stepped back, and squish! the little red bull returned to the earth whence it had come.

The great Nguni beside the truck let loose a mighty sympathetic roar and staled the quad with dung. With a howl, and the manifold sensations of sudden release of many kilopascals of compressed methane, Black Jim and his woman took off into the air. The last they saw of them was a little dust devil that sped erratically across the pot-holed street, raising ash from the ruins of the Prickly Pear as it went. The sound of ghostly cheering, beat of cowhide drum, of a thousand kieries against the cowhide shields; and overall, Gogo's high ululation.

Valiant shook his head. Toby hugged Clementina. But Malibongwe frowned:

'*Hayi!* It's worked for now, Valiant. But there's no guarantee against his return. Forge your new world. Keep to your path. But stay in touch. Serious, my friend. Serious.'

CREPUSCULE

HECTOR BLAINE, AUTHOR, READ OVER what he'd just composed:

In the purple crepuscule, dark figures toiled with burdens on the bank of that oily flood. A miasma stole up from the marshes and lent to their bent forms a spectral guise. A shudder ran through the limbs of Sir Jasper as he watched the clearing of the Lazar House, a spasm not engendered solely by the damp cold of eventide.

He swore and crumpled up the page. His screensaver winked at him and he punched off the computer. He poured cold coffee into his delicious monster, slipped on his sandals, and left his flat. He had to mingle. Every so often Hector needed reality, even just a visit to the supermarket to buy a box of matches, or toothpaste, any pretext to get out and get in touch. He was, by occupation, a writer of neo-Gothic novels. A new taste had emerged, in London, for Gothic fiction. Breakeven, a small but venturesome publisher, had the corner in this market. Every three months Hector Blaine emailed a new book to them from Cape Town. The exchange rate between the pound sterling and the South African rand was hugely in Hector's favour. But how long would it last? It was a wave, a swell, which he must ride before it broke.

But it got to him. His relationships were imperilled. His prose was endangered. His very wits were trammelled and his imagination so heated he could not pass a dog without stretching an imaginary clove of garlic at the beast; could not cross the road without a quick scan for likely funerals and obsequies; desired to wrest every pretty woman from the arms of demons in disguise. Shop dummies were his present phobia, manikins which (he knew) stretched spectral hands and damning fingers at him as he passed, bland features which broke into hideous and fleshless grimaces behind his back. He scurried past the plate-glass front of Truworths and its row of figures in party jeans and cropped tops. Each to him was become a siren, alluring to be sure, but *sans merci*, damned, and damning. Freighted with the soulless ligatures of death.

Hector shook his head and made for Cavendish Square, the Mecca of all shopping malls, the consumer's content, the heartland of thingness, 'What you see is what you get.'

And yet, the multi-storey mall becomes a crenellated castle, a keep and donjon, a great hall filled with junketing of wights and maidens. The escalators are as flying dragons, or mad moving staircases out of opium by Fuseli. Now Hector is a *flâneur* strolling through a city of the plain, a vast and lurid scape of twisting streets and tumbled booths, merchandise from Baghdad and Samarkand, Spanish leather, animals and spices. Instead of modern youth at the mall cinema or eating sushi and pizza in the food hall, Hector sees harlequins. He sees jugglers and pickpockets and masquerades, soothsayers and fakirs, beldams and silver-eared gypsies.

He staggers to Joe's Smoothie Bar. 'Help,' he croaks.

'Bad again, huh?' asks Joe.

'Yup. Pour me a posset, thou swarthy Ethiop. And none of thy wormwood or mummy paste.'

'Your problem is you're Eurocentric. You know that? You gotta chill out, Blaine. Go to Sun City for a weekend. Take a break. You can afford it, am I right?'

The grand fantasy hotel, resort and casino of Sun City in the northern bushveld near the border of Botswana. He once spent some days there, courtesy of an airline travel prize. All that happened was African Gothic. Modjadji the Rain Queen and Haggard's *She*, eldritch thorn trees with a broken moon, drumming and the thud of naked feet of impis, blood and fangs, and febrile sessions with imagined maladies and wasting of the limbs. He had to be sedated and sent back home in a helicopter.

'Doesn't help, Joseph.' He downs his smoothie and sighs.

'I will help you,' says Joe. He reaches to the bottle rack above his counter and hands Hector a business card. 'Go see this dude. Down off Albert Road in Woodstock.'

'Malibongwe Ngingingini. Sangoma. Of global renown. Most ailments sorted. Medical aid rates,' the card declares.

Janice Pekeur was attractive. She had long black hair, brown eyes, a soft light-brown skin, and dimples when she smiled. Her form was sweet and lithe, her arms smooth and round. She was a regular patient of Malibongwe, her plight a kind of aphasia whereby she took things at face value and no more.

'Have a nice day,' said the cashier at the supermarket.

'No thanks,' she replied. 'I've got everything I need for now.'

'Shake on it,' said a satisfied client at the bank, as he signed a loan agreement with Janice. She looked around for salt and pepper.

'So,' said Malibongwe to Janice, 'I see you on Thursday; you bring me a box, you put in this box seven things you own and like. You bring all this and show me. Now go. Go well.'

As she went down the swaying outside stairs that led from Malibongwe's old tenement above Faisal and Abdurahman Parker's pet food shop, Janice noticed the pale-faced earnest young man who climbed up trembling. She saw a sandy-haired number-one haircut, a Woolworths shirt, a pair of chinos, sockless deck shoes, a stainless-steel watch, a face lined with stress, a set of pens in his shirt pocket, eyes red with strain.

Hector, for whom the swaying stairs were twisting into a chimera's spinal cord, clasped the wall and through half-closed bleary eyes gazed upon a fair dark-skinned maiden, kirtled in velvet, silken, sweet beyond desire. 'She was an Abyssinian maid, and upon her dulcimer she played, singing of Mount Abora.' His faint heart stirred with an access of chivalric zeal.

'Yo!' called the sangoma from above. 'Young man! What are you doing?'

Hector had the stair rail in a clinch, as if grappling with a monstrous beast. Janice Pekeur made it to the ground just as the rickety stairs broke from their bracket on the outside of the mouldy wall. Hector rode the tumbling stairs that swayed sideways and came to rest in Malibongwe's loquat tree.

'*Hayi! Umlungu u*-flaming idiot! Mind my loquats, you tsotsi!'

Hector climbed shamefaced down the tree and found his way up to Malibongwe's tenement by ladder and hatch inside the pet food shop. Long-suffering Faisal and Abdurahman Parker showed him how.

Malibongwe sighed. Here's a right one, he thought to himself. He glanced at the precious autochrone. He had a very important interview in half an hour with an inspector from Shamans Sans Frontières. Anna Persens was out. She was always out when Janice came for treatment. His surgery was in a mess. The *dolosse*, the knucklebones, needed to be re-energised. The magic beans were germinating. Fleas from his dog Nostril had got into the stuffed beasts that hung from the ceiling – the bat and hadeda, the leguaan, python, coelacanth and crocodile. Nostril wanted a bath. And the rare collection of tiny winged asphyxes, the stuffed hippogriff, the manticore, all needed their monthly votive chant. IGongqongqo, the fabled beast of local legend, huffed and puffed in its stout cage.

Hector broke into a sweat as he gazed upon the arcana of

Malibongwe's trade. It seemed that all his febrile visions were now laid before him, taunting, a warlock's lair.

'No, no, a mistake. I must go. I – I –'

Malibongwe held him by the wrist, sat him down on a wooden stool, and passed him a glass of buchu brandy.

'Drink, young man. Are you a Believer?'

'Huh?'

'I said, Are you Religious? Do you have a Faith? Do you follow a Path?'

'I, er, I go to St Chrysostom's at Christmas. Anglican.'

'Ah yes. Aidan Almost, canon of St Chrysostom's. I know him well.' He could have added that Canon Almost was a wicked rival when it came to buying old books, but now was not the time. 'Your imagination is overheated, young man. You are hectic. You need to meditate. You need to simplify. Do you have qualms, I meant to say, concerning alternative – or shall we say indigenous – healing?'

'No, no. Do what you must, O Druid.' Hector downed the brandy.

'I have little time. Come back on Thursday. I think I have your answer.'

On the appointed day both Hector and Janice climbed the swaying stairs, newly bolted to the rotten wall.

'*Molo*, Janice. *Molo*, Hector. Welcome both. Anna, kindly stay with me.'

Anna Persens, apprentice and Subaltern, was about to leave as Janice entered the studio. She pouted.

'Janice, show me what you've brought.'

Janice set down a small cardboard box. She unpacked a credit card, a string of clothes pegs, a pen-and-pencil set, a pocket dictionary, and three plaster flying ducks. Malibongwe stared and sighed. 'These are your most special things?'

'Not special, that is, meaning species-specific. But these are things I like and use. Perhaps special as distinct from general, if that is what you mean.'

Malibongwe sighed again. A long way yet to go. He held up the largest of the ducks and squinted at it. Nostril whined and pawed his leg.

'Tell me, Janice, what do you see?'

'Um. Plaster, painted green and brown and white. Likeness of a duck. Roughly thirty centimetres long, wingspan roughly forty.'

Anna smirked.

'Hector?' invited Malibongwe.

'Ah. Yes, I would say so too. Also, also – it skims the surface of the mere. Waterfowl are plentiful among the osiers, and Sir Jasper unhoods his glossy falcon. The bird rises on its great pinions. Soaring, it sights its quarry, and in tightening gyres it descends, then swoops upon the hapless prey. Sir Jasper's waterhound plashes through the fen to retrieve the draggled duck.'

'Hector! You are in serious danger of cliché. Here, try these.' Malibongwe held up the string of clothes pegs.

'Oh. Oh dear. The gibbet. The rope. The crossroads, dry bones and rags that ravel on the icy wind. The ravens. Rattling vertebrae.'

'Janice?'

She dimpled. 'Eleven wooden clothes pegs on a nylon cord about twenty-five centimetres long. One of them has a rusty spring. I should get some more. Do you think plastic ones are better?'

'Oh yes,' prompted the Subaltern, 'and you could colour-code them in the winter evenings.'

'Please, Anna. Now look, you two, Hector and Janice. You are two sides of the same coin. You are obverse and reverse. You are pea and pod. You are hoof and you are horn . . .'

Chalk and cheese, muttered Anna to herself.

'You are sun and moon, you are light and shade, you are the yin and yang. I prescribe collaboration. Anna, pass the potion.'

Malibongwe gave Hector and Janice each a small glassful.

'Religion, my friends, is the Latin for to reconnect. You, Hector, need to reconnect with reality. You, Janice, need to reconnect with your imagination. Reality and imagination are as brother and sister, a conjunction that is imperishable, my friends, and that is made by Love. Thus, through Love, shall you – Janice and Hector – reconnect with what you need. And because this is a divine power, I strongly recommend the Church. You, Hector, said you attend St Chrysostom's. High Church, is it not? And Janice?'

She dimpled again. 'I'm a Methodist. Christened in the Elsies River Society.'

'Methodical, to be sure. But to my mind what you need is a good dose of symbolism. Liturgy. Stained glass. Transubstantiation, I think. High Church accepts that doctrine? Anyway, as Coleridge said of the symbolic, that which in specific lets the universal shine through, or words to that effect. And Janice, take this Hector to the Methodists every now and then. Some simplicity will do him wonders. As for myself, I am an African Zionist. Among other things. Anna, stop your sniggers. Remember how you misbehaved at Moria, and bethink you.'

Malibongwe gave Hector the Cape Town Business Directory and instructed him to learn a page off by heart once a week. He pressed a novel by Ann Radcliffe into Janice's hand, and adjured her to persevere with it. Also a copy of *Vathek* by Beckford. Moreover, Janice was to read the Gospel of St John, Hector to study Leviticus and Deuteronomy.

A week passed.

'I far prefer Leviticus to the Business Directory,' confessed Hector to Janice as they found themselves together on their way to the next session with the sangoma. 'What about you?'

'Beckford is crazy. But St John is something else. It makes sense in a way I can't explain. "The Word became Flesh." Its like, like words being things, and yet a whole lot more than that. Things being words too.'

'Take your homework to the beach,' said Malibongwe. 'Try Noordhoek. I know it's cold this time of year but go in time to see the sunset. This is needful. I'll see you both in three weeks' time – I leave for England tomorrow.'

His two patients gathered their books and drove in Janice's hatchback to the wooded Noordhoek. They drove through meadows down to the long and shining beach. They plodded through the sand with their hamper and their homework. The brief dusk drew benign sea smells from the little fleshy shore plants, the sand was silvered with the ebbing tide, light flecked the golden sky. Hector and Janice laid out a rug and sat down with their books. They took a measure each of potion.

'Sunset is like – like a peeled orange,' tried out Janice shyly. She then remembered that they say the same thing of cellulite.

'It's not really setting. The earth is turning on its axis.'

'Oh, Hector, you are getting better.'

'Dear Janice.'

'Dear Hector.'

And the smiling sun then hid behind the wide horizon, yielding to the silver moon.

EAU-DE-NIL

MALIBONGWE NGINGINGINI AND ANNA PERSENS spent a week in Egypt on their way to Heathrow. From Cape to Cairo – an eight-hour crossing of the length of Africa. Standing beside the old Nilometer, with simple ceremony, Malibongwe poured into the Nile a bottle of votive water from the Liesbeek River that flows into Table Bay.

'Ooph, that was fresh,' came a gurgle from the surface of the river.

'Oh! It's the talking flounder!' exclaimed Anna.

'Yes, who else? This your fellow then?' The flounder stared with rounded eye from the swirling waters. 'Ethiopian, eh? 'Bye for now!'

They wandered down Shia al-Muski, towards the market place and the great Mosque and Madrassa of Al-Azhar. Along with the hectic hoot of cars and cry of vendors, the heat of the northern summer hit them like a fiery blast. They passed shop fronts filled with pastries and with women's shoes like silken silver butterflies. They stepped past wizened men in galabiyahs who squatted on the pavement roasting pigeons or heating plates of kufta for sale, fanning fires of burning corncobs with their pigeon-feather fans. Young backpackers from America hastened by with guidebooks and bottled water. 'Baksheesh, baksheesh,' came the high-pitched cry from beggars. A lean man with wide white smile accosted them: 'Hullo, hullo! Salaam! You are very welcome! I am engineer. Where you come from? What you earn?'

'*Imshi!* Go away, O son of a son of a donkey-driver,' called out another. 'You are no engineer but a backstreet bodger of cheap smelly two-strokes. Pray step this way, O Guests, you very welcome, you drink tea in my father's shop, I show you fine perfumes from Fayum.'

'*La-a!* No, no! He's but a pedlar of extract of ageing camel-gland! You step this way, if you please. You do not need those two. You buy carpet, yes? Very good price, you very welcome.'

The three buskers came to fists in the street. Little autos halted and big men got out, and with much hooting and shouting the argument gusted down Shia al-Muski. Police in their colourful uniforms came up, and joined in. While Malibongwe and Anna retreated, the throng began to slap backs and hug and laugh, and pressed into a smoking café for an afternoon of coffee and hookahs.

'They mean no harm.'

It was their old friend Prozacz, the Gypsy King. He was in Cairo to work on matters of Sufi musicology and dance with a troupe of whirling dervishes.

'Hola! It is good to see you, Your Highness,' said Malibongwe. 'Is Queen Rosalie here too?'

'Ah no. My Rosalie is in Albion. I am here in mufti, if you understand. No form, no ceremony. Simpler to get around. Rosalie has gone on to the conference. I gather you're going too. Oxford will be pleasant in July. More temperate than here, that's for sure.'

He took a long draught of freshly squeezed mango juice.

'And why are you breaking your journey, my friends? Tourism or business?'

'Bit of both. We've never been to Egypt. We're not staying long in Cairo though. I have to see a man out in the desert in the monastery of St Hyacinth and St Proteus.

In the desert monastery of the Monophysite martyrs Hyacinth and Proteus (how they suffered) lived Brother Hermetikos. Now a Coptic monk, he'd once been an antique dealer in Cairo but had met his match in the figure of Cy Koentz, antiquarian from Cape Town and a terrifying driver of a bargain. Cy Koentz had gulled the *Testimony of Barathea* out of Brother Hermetikos. This document, an almost intact scroll from the first century AD written in Aramaic with Hellenistic scholia and an interlinear gloss in Coptic, held the key to many mysteries. Koentz kept it in his safe, to publish when the times were ripe. Mortified by the bad bargain, Hermetikos had renounced all worldly goods and taken holy orders.

Cy Koentz, for all his toughness, had a conscience, and this was troubling him and now denied him sleep. In a passing pageant in his waking dreams moved the many dealers and collectors whom he'd trumped in purchase of rare things. He'd begun a complex plan of restitution to make peace with his soul, a jubilee year of quid pro quo and settling of the karmic debt of anguish.

His part in foiling the attempt on the life of King Prozacz and Queen Rosalie had been indirect, to be sure, but even so it had done some good. Now he sought further to allay the troubles of his soul by sharing various lesser artefacts with the gazumped and aggrieved antiquarians who had dealt with him. He had directories of all the towns and cities where he'd made his many conquests from Ougadougou to Gettysburg, Tripoli to Trieste and Pondicherry. When he learnt that Malibongwe and Anna were to visit Egypt he leapt at the chance of setting things right with his Coptic rival.

Easier said than done: Malibongwe and Anna therefore had to go by taxi to Suez, and from there by bus to the town of Hurghada on the Red Sea coast. Another battered taxi took them in the dry heat out to the cliffs of Gebel el Galâla el Qibliya, from where they must needs go afoot for a kilometre or two, over broken desert rockscape and up the winding path to the monastery itself.

'Oof!' puffed Anna, 'Koentz must be *mal* to make us go here.'

But at last the mountain goat track was done, the great stone fortifications of the monastery loomed up, and they were at the doors. They rang the tinkly bell that hung outside. They rang again, and yet again.

A tousled head popped out above them. 'Brother? Sister? Be ye pilgrims seeking board?'

'Good brother,' called up Malibongwe, 'we come with benison for Brother Hermetikos.'

'Hermetikos?'

'Ay, Hermetikos.'

With reluctant moan the doors inched open and the travellers were received. Their feet were washed, they were given dates and bread and water, and a brother made his sandalled way towards them with a caution: 'Brother Hermetikos has sworn an oath of silence, friends. You may see him in his cell.'

Malibongwe and Anna were taken to their quietist, who rose stiffly from his reed mat and stood before them in his hempen robe. His hair was long and white and tucked into his leather belt. His fingernails were long and twisted, as were his toenails. Wild-eyed, he opened his toothless mouth in amazement, then gestured at the rough wooden bench against the wall. Malibongwe and Anna sat down side by side and smiled reassuringly.

'I – er – I take it you understand English?' ventured the sangoma. 'We are sent by one you knew, who wishes your soul well even as he seeks to ease his own. His name is Koentz, Cy Koentz.'

At the words the hermit reeled and rocked. He flung his hands to his ears and shook his head.

'Ag shame man, he's really upset,' whispered Anna.

'Good brother, be of quiet mind. Cy Koentz has sent us to make peace.' At the name the hermit reeled once more, but less intensely.

'Look, Brother Hermetikos. The man Koentz has sent a gift, a pledge to you.'

From his haversack Malibongwe drew a parcel wrapped in brown paper and string. The old man's fingernails prevented him from opening it, and Malibongwe obliged, taking out a handsome encaustic icon from the third century AD, an image of St George, Mari Ghirghis, Prince of Martyrs. It was a fine thing, the colours bright as yesterday, the detail neatly done, the saint's face a glowing lamp of peaceful strength as he embraced the Princess Sabra, whom he'd rescued from the dragon, the dread crocodile.

Brother Hermetikos clutched it without a word. He took it to his little window and crouched and held it to the light, and touched it to his brow, and to his breast. He fell to silent happy prayer, and somehow years of bitterness and blight were lifting from his seamed and faded face.

They nodded, rose, and left the old man's modest cell as glad tears ran from his rheumy eyes.

'Well, Anna, that's that. And we've got our own task of repatriation to see to when we get to England. I'll tell you more about this when we get there. So much of the ancient world has been ravaged by collectors. Speaking of which, we've just got time to visit Toby's friend in Alexandria.'

Their friend the archaeologist Toby Graaff had given them introductions to his colleague Perlesvaus (Pearly) Hardinghe, Egyptologist and Fellow of Mandeville College, Oxford. Perlesvaus Hardinghe had rooms in Alexandria to escape Cairo's summer heat, and back in the great city Malibongwe and Anna took the train from Ramses Station for a courtesy call, and to view the site of the ancient Pharos.

They found Pearly Hardinghe holding court in a grand and decaying apartment up rue Gérard de Nerval, a block or two back from the wide promenade. Worn shutters hung crazily from the long windows. A sea breeze refreshed what otherwise was deeply melancholy, the perennial sadness of old Alex as it mused upon its glorious past. Youths kicked a football on the wide corniche, and seagulls soared above the mole where Ptolemy's great Pharos once had winked its reassuring guiding light.

Hardinghe opened the door a mere foot or so to let them in and quickly shut it again.

'Nobody following you, if I may ask?' he enquired. His living room was close, heavily scented with cologne, rose water and sandalwood, and shuttered against the brilliant sun. Bands of shadowed light fell across the parquet floor, and lit the broken profiles of Ptolemaic statuary. Old tesserae and scarabs glinted in the sunbeams.

Malibongwe looked sideways at Anna as several urchins and alley cats left the room. Beside the window twitched a lean and pearl-hung lady of very many years. In a corner among potted palms sat another lady, of generous proportions, with tragic eyes and misty veils.

'*Allons!*' cried the thin one by the window as Malibongwe entered. '*Bon Dieu! mon cher* Colonel Lorenzo! From ze desert, yes? 'Ow ze sun has tanned you dark! 'Ave you ze news of my 'usband, le Comte? Is Johnny Turk repulsed? What of dear Farouk and ze court?'

The large one by the potted palms soulfully raised her liquid eyes and dabbed at her frontage with scented kerchief. By her side was a peerless golden chalice filled with chocolate éclairs.

'Aphrodite Yasbec, our dear Diva,' said Perlesvaus, bowing to the fat lady. He turned to the thin one at the window: 'Justine, darling, new people. From Afrique du Sud. A famous analyst, I gather, and his companion. My good friends, this is Justine, la Comtesse d'Entrecôte-au-Lyonnaise.'

Hardinghe was engaged in digging for *ostraka* in the mounds of Antinoë and had much to talk about. He showed them the scratched shards, as well as odd bits of papyrus salvaged from the desert sand.

'And look here, old things,' he said, producing a watermarked sheet with Her Britannic Majesty's coat of arms blazoned at the top. 'Yes. Good quality paper, isn't it? Survived the years intact. Now – you may well think this to be a wine list from the British Embassy. You may well indeed. But you'd be wrong, I suggest. There is a pattern. There is a code. I call it, for the present, the Grand Chablis Code. I see in it the hand of those elusive conspirators, the Intoxicati. The telltale tremors in the forming of the script, the inkblot and the stain, the palimpsest of scratchings and rewritings where errors have been made – *or attempts at concealment*. Don't you think?'

This document was not from the Mounds of Antinoë but from the vast dumps that sprawl across the rose-pink Mokkatam Hills, the dumps that poor Copts trawl through for items of some piastres' value. Hardinghe paid them to bring him specialities among the trash.

'Hm,' reflected Malibongwe. 'Have you tested for invisible ink?'

'Ah!' cried Perlesvaus. He fetched a silver sconce and scorched the paper lightly with a candle. 'Aha! Dear fellow, how clever of you!'

There unfolded slowly in faintest brown the following looped script: 'Angela darling, meet me at the usual place, same time. Yours ever, madly, Dickie.'

La Yasbec dabbed at her eyes and absorbed a chocolate éclair.

'I knew it! I knew it!' cried Perlesvaus. 'Conspiracy most thick!'

Pearly had been expelled from the Intoxicati for an indiscretion in his undergraduate days. It hadn't been much more, back then, than a small exclusive 'varsity dining club; but since their carefree youth most of the members had distinguished themselves.

Madame la Comtesse d'Entrecôte-au-Lyonnaise coughed. '*Mon cher le Comte*, *never* would he stoop to use the ink invisible. Bold! But he was bold and brave! Ah, the sonnets that he wrote to me, *ce qu'il était un symboliste! O, les années perdues, perdues!*'

'Symbols, Justine?' enquired Perlesvaus, quivering with interest.

'You would not comprehend,' she replied with some hauteur. She turned her back to him and scribed a hasty cipher in the air.

Madame Sosostris, famous clairvoyant – hundred per cent Cairene, though more parts Smyrna Greek and French than Egyptian – drew apart the beaded curtain of her summer lodgings and stared out from her mashrabiyah balcony on the other side of the empty boulevard. She allowed her veil to slip, to let the sun glint briefly on the silver coins strung round her neck, her startling blue eyes to flash across the street.

'Pah!' spat Madame la Comtesse d'Entrecôte-au-Lyonnaise with vigour. 'La Sosostris? *Merde!*' she snapped. '*La vieille*, she is but a fraud! Le Vicomte, he knew this well! Why does she signal to you, Perlesvaus? Why? My nerves are bad. Yes, bad! Do not ask her in.'

Perlesvaus fetched out his slide rule from among a pile of scarabs, the instrument that would assign numbers to the new-found letters and crack the Chablis Code. If this was in truth the work of the Intoxicati, Pearly might hold in his hands the fate of the West – but that's another story. The diva reached into the chalice for another éclair while la Comtesse made rude gestures through the window at the crinkled pouting *moue* of Madame Sosostris. A long-standing rivalry, clash of jealous hearts, distrust, and more . . .

Malibongwe and Anna caught each other's eye and slipped out, unnoticed, and after the heated perfumed room drew lungfuls of fresh seaside air.

'*Siestog*,' reflected Anna.

'*Ewe*. Yes indeed. This is what happens to expatriates. The diaspora. Cramped rooms and ancient feuds, nerves and fading memories.'

'Could it be the heat?' asked Anna.

'Possibly.' A yellow dog trotted over to the shady side of rue Gérard de Nerval. 'More likely just the upshot of lost years. Sawdust and isolation. You see, Anna, the soft fruits of the colonial world. Rootless folk, out of time, out of place. Hermetikos is OK. These ones, Pearly and his friends, live in unsustainable illusion – but come, who are we to take it from them? We've got other work in any case. Let's go.'

Musing on the melancholy scene, Malibongwe and Anna headed for the station, and for Cairo.

ZEBRA CROSSINGS

'WE'LL HAVE TO RETURN TO EGYPT,' Malibongwe said to Anna. 'There're a lot of things I need to work through here. Apart from the Intoxicati, though, thank you very much! Egypt holds the key to many mysteries. Our lineage may well have its roots by the Nile. It rises in levels like the river sediment, it ebbs and flows, it lies here in layer on layer – Abbasid and Fatimid and Marmeluke, Copt and Greek and Roman, thousands of years of Pharaohs – here is the very meaning of crosscultural encounter and exchange.'

'*Jirre*. You been reading the guidebook?'

'The Book of Life, Anna. The Book of Ra.' Malibongwe was in scholarly mood. 'It's not merely crosscultural. The Egyptians were specialists at Crossing Over. You know – from Realm to Realm. Just look at that then.'

Their taxi, at breakneck speed, flew past what the Cairenes term the City of the Dead – kilometres of walled necropolis with its cramped mausoleums.

'The pyramids. The thousand tombs. The portals to eternity,' Malibongwe commented.

'Pyramids? Very big! Very old!' cried the taxi man, hooting madly as a flock of sheep crossed the highway. He raced on to the airport.

Crete lay like a toy island far below them. The stewardess in leopard-skin livery came round with boiled eggs and Oros. 'Orange or raspberry?' High Five was a budget airline that catered for the recent boom in Africa tourism.

'Flying wasn't always like this,' said Malibongwe, still in thoughtful mood, as he peeled his egg. 'Just think – down there on Crete, the old craftsman Daedalus and his son Icarus. They had to make their own wings to escape from the island. And Phaethon, he drove the horses of the chariot of the sun and also ended up in the sea.'

'*My magtig.*' Anna hung on to her seat and peered down at the shining Mediterranean where toy ferries plied to Cyprus and Piraeus.

'Hard boiled or soft?' called the stewardess as she moved down the aisle. Malibongwe continued his reflections. 'And did you know, Anna, the ancient culture down there on Crete – the Mycenaean – the roots of all the glory that was Greece – it came across the sea from Egypt. Africa, yes Africa, the Africa of Numibian and Hyksos, was the root of it. The old kingdoms that ran across the continent down to Timbuktu and the Dogon. Think of it.'

Malibongwe's mind was fastened on diasporas, the Africa of then and now, the great changes wrought by time. Where once the votive songs and images of gold had sailed to Knossos, latterly – for some three centuries – the people of the continent had crossed the seas not with singing priests and cunning craftsmen but with beat of slaver's drum and crack of whip and clank of chain. The cradle was become a grave. When, oh when, and how, to kindle reawakening? Five days hence, Malibongwe was to address the seventieth International Conference of Shamans and Traditional Healers on this very topic: a spiritual Renaissance for Africa.

The zebra-striped High Five aircraft soared across the plains of Macedonia and so to Middle Europe, on over Germany and France, over the Channel, and at last sank down to the massed rooftops of Middlesex and the rain-drenched runways of Heathrow. Pressing their faces to the window, they made a game of spotting other High Fives, and there they were, lots of them, in bright African livery. It cheered them to see this branding on the tarmac so far from home, and they took the tube to Paddington with lifted spirits.

Booked into their bed-sit, they went out to explore the city. Oxford Street was packed as usual, a fine June day after the rainfall of the previous night, and crowds of shoppers jostled on the pavements. The red buses nudged their way past Selfridges with its great statue of Isis on the facade, and the pair wandered down through Mayfair and the Burlington Arcade to Piccadilly, the Royal Academy and the Ritz. It was Anna's first time abroad and she stopped at the many hole-in-the-wall counters which operated between these national institutions, to purchase plastic bobby helmets, postcards and jester hats.

There was something about London, Malibongwe thought, something reassuring – in a volatile world, a darkling plain, a world of struggle and alarm, this great city stood stable. Not only for Londoners born and bred, but also for the many foreign refugees who found their way to the metropolis as a haven from their woes. A crosscultural city, a city of change and interchange enabled by its abiding certainties . . . But then his attention switched to Anna, who'd thoughtlessly animated a zebra crossing. 'Hola! *Anna!* Whatever have you done?'

The zebra crossing stood up on hoofed feet. It snorted, shook its head, and looked around. Two people who were halfway across found themselves clinging to its mane and tail. A policeman leapt back as the creature reared at him and threw the pedestrians. It was alarmed by the hooting buses and taxis. It pranced a little and then galloped up Shaftesbury Avenue with a stream of traffic, Anna and police officers in its wake. The chase swerved down the Charing Cross Road, heading for Leicester Square. A panto horse joined the dash through London's theatreland but split apart at the seams. Then into Trafalgar Square, and Malibongwe halted, engulfed in a crowd of protesters. What a mêlée! Where's Anna? Where's that zebra crossing? Malibongwe fought for breath and surveyed the scene.

'*Heito* Potato!' shouted a bespectacled black African at the head of the protesters. He had a stethoscope around his neck. 'We want anti-retrovirals! AIDS is not a myth!'

'*Heito* Potato!' shouted the crowd. 'Anti-retrovirals for Africa! Free anti-retrovirals, now!'

Malibongwe saw that the protest was going on outside the South African Embassy, and the penny dropped. Official denialism in South Africa about HIV and AIDS had conveniently relieved the state of rolling out anti-retroviral medicines; instead, so the Cabinet indicated, people could simply eat more African potatoes, as well as garlic and beetroot. Since this had no effect on folk with full-blown AIDS, even Malibongwe and his fellow traditional healers, notwithstanding their commitment to herbal remedies, understood the need for ARVs.

Paranoia, and hence denialism, Malibongwe reflected as he scanned the crowd for a glimpse of Anna or the zebra crossing, was by no means limited to such as the expatriate Hardinghe and his conspiracy theories. Even governments, otherwise intelligent and progressive, can readily suffer from it.

Ah, there they were! He spotted the elusive figures caught up in a maul at the other side of the Square. Oh no! They're off again!

Malibongwe fought his way through the crowd and found himself in the broad expanse of Whitehall. Anna was on the galloping zebra's back, struggling to keep her seat. Police were thick as bluebottles in her wake as she headed for the heartland of the British civil service. Past the old Banqueting Hall, the Admiralty, the startled sentries at the entrance to Horse Guards – and then the zebra snorted and gave up its pell-mell flight. There was a crowd of pinstriped civil servants on the pavement. They pointed with their fountain pens and murmured with agitation.

The Metropolitan Police formed a cordon around the zebra crossing. A Land Rover raced down Whitehall with a squad of Guardsmen armed with automatic rifles. Poor Anna. More sirens, more police cars, more civil servants. A van from the RSPCA was stopped and turned back as the police set up their roadblock.

Malibongwe approached. Anna was gesticulating in a circle of police. The zebra stood still, its flanks heaving, steam rising, its tail switching. The granite block behind them said 'Foreign and Commonwealth Office'. Malibongwe realised then that the animated zebra had a mission of some sort. He stood listening – this was Anna's mess and she must sort it out. He strained to hear her words over the bemused buzzing of the civil servants.

'No, I'm *not* from the circus,' protested Anna. 'And it's nothing to do with the demonstration in Trafalgar Square. You leave them out of this. I just made a mistake and I'm sorry. Up there – London Main Street – where the shops all are – how must I know the name of the road? I'm a tourist! South African, here's my passport. Yes, I've got a right to be here, haven't I? No, I'm not a refugee. What do you mean asylum? You think I'm *mal?*'

The policemen scratched their heads.

'*Kyk*, this thing I do, I just wanted to try it out overseas, OK? Yes, animation. You know? Oh for goodness' sake! Yes, I know I can't go animating zebra crossings in the heavy traffic.'

A man in shaded glasses and a dark suit took over the interrogation.

'Ja, it *is* unusual, hey. *Jirre*, you from MI5? No, I can't say how it works. Hey, I'll just do it back again. No, I haven't got a gun; I'm not a flippin' gangster, man!'

So many questions. Could Anna pull it off on her own? This would be an important chance for her to gain more *ukuthwala*.

Anna went up to the zebra and caressed its neck. She took it by the muzzle and whispered into its ear. Now she seemed to be listening to the beast. It nuzzled her shoulder and they remained in a huddle for a few minutes.

'OK, everybody.' She turned to the policemen. 'I can do this for you, but first the zebra's got a message. It's got to say this thing, then it'll lie down nice and quiet on the road again. OK?'

Malibongwe's heart leapt into his mouth as he saw sharpshooters stealing into position on the Foreign Office roof. *Please* get this right, Anna!

'The zebra says it's talking from experience.' Anna spoke up clearly for the crowd to hear. Malibongwe was impressed; his apprentice was certainly growing up.

'The zebra says it's seen a lot in its time. It says every day it sees things it must talk about. The big thing is getting people across the street. They get knocked down. They are too scared to cross. They come from overseas from other cultures and they don't know what side the traffic goes on in England. They are confused, far from their home.'

Somebody in the crowd hemmed and hawed. Someone else murmured in sympathy.

'They need protection. They've got human rights like everyone. Shame, the children are the worst, hey. The zebra says the Foreign Office must respect the refugees. Somalis. Egyptians. Afghanis. *Jirre*, he's got a long list. Chechens. Zimbabweans. Tibetans. He's seen them all. He says it's easier to cross the Jordan or Limpopo than to go around in England. He says visas are a problem. *Ag, mense*, he's *rêrig* proud to be an English zebra and he's proud of his country's institutions and its defence of freedom; but speaking as an English zebra, he wants the FO to do something about it. And he doesn't mean Eff Off, OK? He means the Foreign Office.'

There were scattered cheers but also disapproving cries of 'Shame!' from among the onlookers, who began to argue among themselves.

Anna had finished speaking. She stroked the zebra's head gently, and eased it down onto its knees. Then the haunches.

She squatted beside it, stroking it all the while, and whispering in its ear. She turned to the watching crowd. 'Ja, and he says he needs a bit more paint.'

She continued to whisper and stroke, and as she did, so the gentle creature sank to the tar, its handsome stripes running true across the road in black and white. She knelt silently beside the crossing while the crowd quietly applauded, conscious of the solemnity of the moment.

The civil servants drifted away, debating. The police remained, writing hard in their notebooks. While they were thus preoccupied, Malibongwe stepped up and gave Anna his hand. He raised her to her feet.

'Anna, that was terrific. *Kunjani wena?* You all right? Let's go, shall we?'

PINK ALABASTER

Malibongwe was no stranger to London, but no frequent visitor either. He stood anew in awe at the bustle and variety. He loved the red buses with their turbaned drivers, the boxlike black taxis so like the Nguni cows he knew in the Eastern Cape. He smiled at the Cockney backchat. Enjoyed again the rambling heights of Hampstead Heath, the Henry Moores among the trees, the view down over the broad city basking in high summer.

He was specially fond of the Thames and its lower reaches where the vessels, and their commerce, sailed out to the farthest parts of the earth as they had done for centuries past. His mind's eye saw old Tudor barques and caravels, East Indiamen, the Blackwall frigates, the graceful clippers, Hanseatic barquentines and brigs, the lumbering Thames barges, schooners and yawls and pilot boats; and the steamers, rusty buckets back from Candy or the Coast of Coromandel with their spices; cruisers and their squadrons; a bright flagship put in from Malta; the greyhounds of the sea, the transatlantic liners. All these Malibongwe sensed and in them felt a greatness, not his own nor that of London, but of all people.

But this tide had ebbed, and now it was Heathrow, and an easy coming-and-going, and crowds all in coats and beanies and squashy jester caps and rugby scarves, New Zealanders for Twickenham, South Africans for Hammersmith and tiny bed-sits, Georgians from Tbilisi, and Iranians and Croats and Sudanese and Somali refugees, Italian opera-singers and migrant chefs, students heading for the snug basement bongo-sessions at the School of Oriental and African Studies, a diverse hugger-mugger fed from Heathrow by the tube and like little platelets and corpuscles floating through the arteries of the city. This he felt and knew. His own blood thrilled.

Enough of that. There was Anna, struggling out of a taxi with a mass of parcels. She was wrapped in a gorgeous fur, there was something bright in her hair (surely not a tiara?) and she scattered little beribboned parcels of parfumerie and lingerie as she pressed the bell. On whose credit card were these set down?

'Hau, Anna! What have you been doing?'

'Oh, just some things. You know. Bric-à-brac.' A platinum brooch with an enamelled face of the late Princess of Wales bounced down the area stairs, and a silk scarf with the colours of the Union Flag caught on the iron railing. 'I got a DVD of the Spice Girls too. In concert.' A frilly crimson thong slipped from her bag and she had the grace to blush.

Malibongwe sighed.

They made tea in their tiny bed-sit, dunking the heating element in each mug in turn. Anna popped a Harrods Mozartkugel in her mouth and tried her vowels like Professor Higgins's Eliza: 'Air, hellair. Pleased to meet you, your Grace. This is so lovely, is it not? Are not the crumpet very excellent?'

'Your concord, my dear,' Malibongwe corrected her gently while chocolate ran down her chin. '*Is* not the crumpet, Anna. A collective noun. Now listen carefully. The reception is at South Africa House at six. There will be speeches. We do not speak until we are spoken to. I receive my decoration at seven. Here, see the programme for yourself.'

They arrived in Trafalgar Square at a quarter to the hour, and were ushered into the embassy. Malibongwe wore formal evening dress. Anna matched his dinner jacket with a Burlington Bertie ensemble, a richly embroidered waistcoat and a pair of impeccable Doc Martins. In the vestibule, beneath a vast tapestry with a fanciful map of Africa that once hung in Cecil Rhodes's study, a string quartet played kwela and strains of 'Manenberg'. Anna did a little jive as the hired butler, dressed in a Mandela shirt, gingerly removed her coat.

'Malibongwe, my dear fellow,' gushed the Ambassador. '*Kunjani? Wamkelekile*, my dear friends, you are very welcome. So this is Anna? A signal honour.'

There was no mention of the events of the day before. A very good South African sherry was served, from the Calitzdorp district in the Little Karoo. A second string quartet performed updated classics in the gallery beneath the murals by Pierneef and Juta. Anna took her third sherry, swaying slightly to a syncopated barcarole. Pierneef's glowing cubist mural of thorn trees and golden koppies lost its focus as she downed a fourth. Juta's epic view of the Voortrekkers, straining with their ox wagons over the ramparts of the Drakensberg, lurched as she felt her legs go rubbery. The barcarole was become like a heaving sea. Too many Mozartkugeln, she giggled to herself.

The president of Shamans Sans Frontières stepped forward to make the presentation. The Ambassador beamed. The string quartet broke into 'Nkosi Sikelel' iAfrika'. Toasts were drunk in hanepoot muscadel. As she went down, the last thing Anna saw was the broad ribbon of the Supreme Order of the Aloe Vera, so handsome as it lay on Malibongwe's crisp white breast.

'Malibongwe, are you there? Is Mademoiselle Anna feeling better? Please forgive my insistence at this early hour, but it is a matter of some urgency.'

Anna groaned and hid in her sleeping bag on the sofa. Malibongwe unlocked the door.

'Ah! Monsieur Therapin! An honour indeed.'

It was the president of Shamans Sans Frontières, Georges Therapin from Longueuil in Quebec.

'Malibongwe, *mon frère*. A notable evening, *n'est ce pas?* Forgive this early intrusion, but the professor cannot wait.'

A tiny man in morning coat and pinstripes bobbed at Therapin's elbow. 'My dear fellow!' piped the tiny professor. 'Only you can be of help. The direst consequences . . .'

And so it turned out that the predicted rising of the Middle East was on the move. Not Hamas. Not the Shi'ites and Sunnis of Iraq. Not the Lebanese militia. No, it was an uprising of the artefacts of the eastern Mediterranean: Minoan Greek, Etruscan, Chaldean and Sumerian, Egyptian and Boeotian. In sympathy, no doubt, for the beleaguered people of Iraq; also, at root, a bubbling up of long-repressed dreams dreamt by the exile: dreams of olive groves, dreams of marshes where the duck and crocodile dwell; dreams of dolphins in the isthmus, of palm and papyrus, of donkeys and delight. The return of the repressed, bursting through forms of clay and amber and basalt and alabaster. Life such as no sculptor dared to envisage, writhing and swelling beneath the long-passive matter of the ages.

'And what's more, it's going to endanger the Chinese jade, the collection of lacquer, the Venetian glass. And as for the set of early Wedgwood! Oh my word, my word! And what if all these arise in sympathy?'

'Where's this going on?'

'Sir John Soane's Museum. Lincoln's Inn Fields. Quick. The rebellion will be moving on to the antique dealers in Coptic Street, and then – and then the British Museum! All of Bloomsbury will be aflame.'

Malibongwe knew that time was of the essence. He mixed Anna her anti-retrovirals and a Bloody Mary, pulled on his corduroys, and dashed after the president and the professor. Rebellion? *Hmm.* More like a necessary adjustment, surely; an inevitable reaction against imbalance? But it could prove ugly.

Sir John Soane's Museum lies in the four-storey townhouse once owned by this eighteenth-century savant and early Royal Academician. It is a delight of encyclopaedic taste. In the basement is the skeleton of a Benedictine monk. The stairwell is cased with plaster casts from antique statuary. Walls are hung with oils by Hogarth, contemporary and confidant of the old connoisseur. These were not the problem.

Malibongwe stepped past the trembling curator. His wild gaze was met with riot. An ancient Zoroastrian, knife raised, held a bellowing bull by its forelock. On a silken carpet, a bowl of fine chalcedony lay within inches of the beast's pawing hoof. Three naked girls from Knossos vied to leap across the bull's broad back while peasants tied its horns with wreaths of amaranth and olive. A constable of the Metropolitan Police tried to handcuff an alarming priest of Memnon. The cuneiform tablets chattered angrily in Sumerian on the mantelpiece and somewhere timbrels and sistra were beaten in a pulsing frenzy. Chaldean temple prostitutes tumbled down the stairs, singing as they greeted a host of maenads. A vine-leaved bearded satyr broke into the collection of old wine and poured himself a silver Regency goblet of the musty draught. A proud pharaoh stood and made to speak 'My name is Ozymandias – ' but he was overwhelmed by a mad rush of temple servants of the Akhenaton heresy.

At the uproar old Silenus stirred in his hirsute sleep. Already, Malibongwe noticed, an exquisite jade Chinese horse appeared to snort and toss its frozen head; already a porphyry Buddha's belly seemed to quiver, his ears prick up at the unaccustomed din. If the furthest Orient were to come to Levant's aid! If all of Indus were to rise! Babylon and Persia . . . And then Arabia, and Morocco, and Chad and Mwana-Matapa and the kingdoms of old Africa . . . For a moment Malibongwe paused and his heart reached out and swelled.

But a harpy clawed at his hair, and a centaur seemed about to smash the window. Erinyes flew maddeningly about the ceiling, and a jackal-headed figure from a canopic jar rose with cold intent. Atropos glided in with her shears, and Ra seemed mad with lust for living souls. A pink alabaster fairy, art nouveau, flew in the window with tiny violence at Malibongwe and he caught and pocketed the wriggling creature. Tinkerbell! Wrong epoch. Time to stop the party, he thought. He wished Anna were there, with her flair for animation – and for stopping it.

He strode to a long-case clock. Spun the hands. Back, back, one hour, two, three, four, eight, twelve . . .

'Now listen, all of you!' Malibongwe cleared his throat. 'Aeons come and aeons go. You have no idea what's going down these days. The Age of Aquarius, my friends. Granted there's much hurt; granted these folk in the West have done much harm; but you won't get it sorted by this kind of anarchy. One imbalance isn't cured by yet another. Yes, you, you silly maenad, and you, you ancient priest of Memnon. Put down that paperweight. Take it easy now. *Kahle, kahle*.'

It was a bad move. The singing just grew wilder, the threats more dire. Hogarth's Bad Apprentice smirked from his oil-on-board. The Good Apprentice held his hands to his head.

Back in their bed-sit Anna showered and made herself a cup of tea. 'Aitsa! That was bad.' The room no longer spun around her. She gathered her wits. 'Malibongwe's got the recognition he deserves. But why did I go and behave like a flipping gentoo on the make, like a Long Street *dronkie* kerbside girlfriend?'

She drank her herbal tea, *ubulau*, the cleanser. As her mind was washed, something glimmered in the corner of her eye. There flitted scenes of gorgeous riot. Sunshine and dark groves, crystal rocks and golden corn, bright limbs that shone and wrapped around lithe bodies. All the world of root and leaf, bare feet, flashing eyes, laughter.

'*Jirre!*' she reflected. 'That's now lekker.' But beside the phone in their bed-sit lay the cheap photocopied adverts for call girls from around London Town. And the rush of traffic in the Tottenham Court Road never ceased. And the TV showcased rival boy bands and girl bands who pretended to play guitar while electronic music belted from their consoles. And the newscast reported cordite-girt bombers that ran yelling into knots of people on Iraqi streets, and oil went up in price.

'If only,' she thought. The vision came and went, like subliminal advertising, in her mind's eye. 'If only we could clean it all, get wise. Yes! And I had to *sommer* go and get drunk on Malibongwe's big night. Stupid!'

Neverland was playing on another channel. 'Ja-nee. Peter Pan and Wendy. Me and Malibongwe.'

Then something happened. Pan spoke to her. A voice ever young and ever old, a deep croak and light laughing. A voice wrapped in all the senses, the whispering hot scent of gardenia and jasmine, the bloom on the surface of a peach. Or almond blossom and thick billets of leathery vanilla pod.

The voice spoke – or sang – of light among the leaves, of clear waters and rippled shade, of storm and sun and moon, and man and woman. It sang of the dryad in the pool, the nymph laughing in the golden corn. It sang of the true heart that honoured animals and the life of trees. It then sang sad words that spoke of loss, and laboured life, and bitter hate, and strife. The fallen groves, the acid rain and lifeless ocean, the tar and gushing oil.

Anna sat and wondered.

Then, from the TV screen: *Neverland* – and Johnny Depp as Peter Pan saying, 'Anna? Anna! Are you listening?' Depp flashed his white smile, flicked his wrists, and levelled his dark eyes at her. 'Don't be silly. Stop shrieking. I'm not a rock star, dear. Got a message for you: Anna. It's all gone, almost. You can help to get it back, you and your friend, with all the others. Will you help?'

'Oooh, yes!'

'Um. Like, patch up this world? Ride a dolphin to fetch the King and build his throne? If you know what I mean?'

'Wow!'

'You got it, Anna. Do you give your word?'

'Oh, yes! Oh, for sure! I do!'

The image of Johnny Depp smiled and faded. The TV shifted to a newscast, a scene in London – a terraced house in a handsome square, a police cordon, and there was Malibongwe! Pointing straight at her, gesturing with his hand for her to come; asking her.

'Oh, I do, I do, I do! I'll help to fix the Kingdom!'

On a marble urn a procession of citizens and priests froze in their eternal round. The bull they led was docile as it melted back into the contours of the vase. Ozymandias collapsed into broken profile, and with a clatter the canopus jars clamped their lids back on. The cantering of hoofs died down. The maenad gave Malibongwe a long and knowing look as she slowly climbed the stairs to her cold frieze. He stared down the muscular priest of Memnon, who sheathed his nasty-looking sword.

'*Allons!* That was close!' Georges Therapin, president of Shamans Sans Frontières, peered in from the threshold, the little professor at his side.

'I'll say. Now look, leave the clock at yesterday and close the museum for a week or two. Let them settle down.'

Strolling through Hyde Park as they waited for the bus from Marble Arch to Oxford, Malibongwe and Anna noted the more recent statuary. The Duke of Wellington. The Artillery Memorial. A sadly different world, Malibongwe thought. Noble, yes. But not with that archaic joy. A world of power and repression. The muffled drum. The stony sacrifice. But the elms and chestnuts were golden-green, and dogs gambolled among the flushed sun-worshippers. Red buses came down Kensington Gore. Only, Peter Pan was no longer where he used to stand in Kensington Gardens. His gaudy plinth was vacant. A faint fluting and light laughter drifted across the Serpentine. The rose-pink alabaster fairy in Malibongwe's pocket seemed to flutter. He squeezed Anna's hand and smiled a quiet smile.

SAGE GREEN

MALIBONGWE STUMBLED UP from the Pitt Rivers Museum with a blinding headache. He felt in his oatmeal linen suit for an aspirin, but Anna silently passed him a wad of willow bark to chew.

'*Hayi*,' muttered Malibongwe, 'what a jumble sale they've got in there. And everything goes *ukuthethathethana* in its own language, like the tower of Babel with the scaffolding falling down.'

Malibongwe's powers were intensified in the museum, among the collected fetishes of a thousand cultures crammed into the dark interior of that most Victorian of Oxford institutions. Malibongwe Ngingingini was taking a short break from the seventieth annual International Conference of Shamans and Traditional Healers. After the recent events in the Sir John Soane Museum he had good reason for headache.

He looked back at the Ruskinian Gothic brick façade of the University Museum that housed the Pitt Rivers collection. Emerging up into the pale sunshine were the other conference delegates, some in suits, some in the sealskins and beadwork and woven shawls of their calling. There was Malibongwe's friend from Eleusis, Alexikakos (Lexie) Kyriakos, and there the Inuit Kingminggoarkulluk, adorned with walrus tusks, and the stately Algonquin, Grey Wolf, Son of Manitou, in his feather headdress. Rosalie the Gypsy Queen grasped Anna's hand and scanned her palm benevolently as the group made their way to Mandeville College for afternoon tea.

In the Master's Garden the international shamans made small talk, some shuffling decks of Tarot cards, some speculating over tea leaves, some debating the merits of ginger, ginseng and ginko root as an alternative to Lapsang Suchong or Earl Grey. The garden itself had a noted herbarium, first planted by Grey Friars in the fourteenth century, and celebrated in the sixteenth with an illustrated herbal attributed to a cousin of Culpeper. Malibongwe moaned and dunked willow bark in his tea. The weight of centuries oppressed him. Every golden Cotswold stone, every slim Jacobean brick, every gnarled root chattered to his inner ear: the secret voices of things, the akashic record of the material world, rendered audible to those few with the gift of mystic hearing, only too audible in this thickly layered city.

Through the static and chatter from the cobblestones around his chair, and the chuckle of water sprites in the Cherwell that flowed beside the Master's Garden, Malibongwe realised that Lexie Kyriakos, in his usual dithyrambic and archaic fashion, was addressing him.

'Orpheus, do you realise? You are Orpheus; and this dear woman,' gesturing at Anna Persens, 'why, she is your Eurydice! I see you rise from the museum. You come up into the light like Orpheus, like Orpheus o'er the threshold, only you have beaten the ancient curse. You look back at her, yet she is not snatched back down again! She steps across the threshold at your side, you enter the world of light together! Orpheus and Eurydice, my dear friends! Orpheus and Eurydice now triumph o'er the dark gods that moil for aye below! *Io, xairete, xairete toisi!*'

'Funny you should say that,' Malibongwe said faintly, his teeth gritted against a migraine. 'Orpheus who with his lyre charms the savage breast of . . .'

Anna, apprentice, Subaltern and sceptic, shrugged as she nibbled a muffin. Malibongwe couldn't make music to save his life; she had hidden his mouth organ where even divination would not find it, in the lead plumbing of his old tenement back home.

'I need to find an Orpheus while I'm in Oxford,' continued the sangoma with dignity, through Anna's plashing thought-waves.

'Tell me more.' The Greek raconteur sensed a good story.

Teshu Lama from Such-zen in Tibet wandered into the tea party with his snuff gourd and his begging bowl. 'Ah, my child,' he beamed at Anna, 'and you who were once my *chela* in another life, Little Friend of All the World, sit you here scoffing chocolate muffins!' With her dark eyes she stared at the lank and seamed old man in his woollen gabardine blanketing. These shamans are crazy, she thought. First they call me Eurydice, then some half-baked Pathan *klonkie*. I'm just me, thank you very much; and she smoothed her long legs sheathed in black stovies, and cast her eyes over the fine surface of her Doc Martins.

'See this book,' Malibongwe said to Lexie Kyriakos. 'Show him, Anna. I found this copy in Cranfield's in the High.' Anna passed a handsome octavo volume to the Greek.

'Hmm. *Frank Lascelles, Our Modern Orpheus. Essays in Honour of the Pageant Master of Empire*. Published by Oxford University Press, 1932. Edited by the Earl of Darnley. What's all this about, then? And why "Orpheus"?'

'Have a look, *umhlobo wam*. This man, Lascelles, he put on public performances, historical pageants, all over the world. See: Oxford in 1907, Quebec 1908, Cape Town 1910, the coronation durbar in Delhi 1911, London in 1912, and so on and so forth. I've got to find his house – I know he lived in Oxfordshire, a little place called Sibford Gower, where he was Lord of the Manor. Like a tribal leader, an Nkosi.'

'But why? What's that to you, my dear Malibongwe? Assuming it still exists.'

Teshu Lama levitated from his wicker chair beside them, chuckling quietly in the ecstasy of meditation. Anna grabbed the old man's teacup before it hit the cobbles.

'You've seen the Pitt Rivers collection,' the sangoma said. 'You know how it is – those Inca mummies, the Caribbean obeah, the spears and darts with dried *muti* on their blades, the corn dollies, the little ships of the dead that have been blown so far off course, the distaffs and spinning wheels that rattle and hum no more, the shrivelled scalps of Iroquois and

Huron, the prayer mats, the earthenware – '

Crash! went Teshu Lama, landing among the tea things.

They continued their conversation in the calm of the senior common room.

'Lascelles was the producer of these outdoor public performances. The one in Oxford was his first, to mark the eighth century of the founding of the city. Rudyard Kipling was there, and Mark Twain, all sorts of royalty and so forth, and by and large Lascelles came in for a great deal of recognition.

'This was his big break. He was created an honorary Druid of the Isis Lodge by a contingent of Latter Day Druids from Oxfordshire and Wiltshire who took part in the Eothred at the solstice that summer.

'But here's the point. In Quebec, in 1908, he was made an honorary chieftain of the Iroquois. They gave him the title of Tehonikonraka, which means, I think, Man of Many Resources. They clad him in wampum and a headdress of eagle's feathers. Then, in Cape Town, in 1910, he was made an honorary chief of the BaSotho, and they called him Rakalello, Man of Marvellous Ideas, in rough paraphrase. And they gave him a silver casket, and in this silver casket was the tooth of an ancient BaSotho priest-diviner known to his people as Raka. This tooth Lascelles then wore around his neck on a silver chain. Now the people want it back. Lascelles is no more – it's no use to him. I've been asked to seek out Raka's tooth and return it to his village. That's my brief.'

Big Bev the herbalist from Hammersmith interrupted Malibongwe with her customary query: 'Do you do floaters, folks?' And the shamans decided tea was over.

After dinner Boaz, the Chaldean astrologer, drew Malibongwe aside. Teshu Lama joined them. Boaz took a sip of port and spoke. 'My friend Malibongwe, let me assure you of the earnest of your brief.'

Boaz cut a cigar and shot his cuffs. He removed his dark

glasses. He smoothed his double-breasted jacket and adjusted the pocket kerchief. Malibongwe waited. Teshu Lama wriggled and his bright eyes gleamed.

'Your country, my friend,' continued Boaz. 'The time of nation states is at an end. Yet your country is so young; like Anna. So very young. You realise that from the time when your country was made into a nation to the time you were freed from apartheid, that was exactly 84 years?'

'*Ewe*. South Africa became a unified nation state in 1910. Eighty-four years later we ended the apartheid system. What's your point, Brother Boaz?'

'Hee-hee', giggled Teshu Lama. 'It's the new planet! Tell him, Boaz.'

'Uranus, my friend.'

'Your anus! Your anus! Get it?' the lama chortled. 'Cleanse the body, eh?'

Boaz coughed and returned to his topic. 'Uranus. First named Herschel after the man who discovered it in 1781. And by the by, Herschel worked for some years in Cape Town.'

'What goes around comes around,' nodded Teshu Lama bursting into laughter.

'Uranus is the planet of social change. Of revolution. Slow-moving and epochal, Uranus leaves certain details unattended. You, Malibongwe, like many others, must help to pick up the pieces. I felt obliged to point this out, my friend. Now, won't you take a glass of port?'

Malibongwe and Anna wandered off, down Longwall Street and Holywell, into Broad Street. The stone Emperors on their pillars outside the Sheldonian gave low wolf-whistles as Anna passed, and she glared at them. The Earl of Pembroke, on his plinth in his half-armour and tights, had already pinched her when they visited the Bodleian. She wanted more respect from these ancient gentlemen, and she wasn't getting it. On the other hand, Cecil Rhodes in his niche on the façade of Oriel wasn't interested in girls and winced as she passed by. Anna had desires too and she wanted to mingle with the living at a nightclub in the quarter known as Jericho; but such things had to wait. First, she and Malibongwe had their mission, to seek the destiny of Raka's tooth.

The two caught the train to Banbury, then a local bus north-west into the leafy Cotswolds. Sturdy old farmhouses lay in folds in the hills, screened by deep hedgerows and avenues of beech and chestnut. All was peaceable. They read their guidebooks. Until – 'Yo!' cried Malibongwe. 'Stop the bus!'

Anna woke from an uneasy sleep in which vast statues moved and menaced.

'Stop! Stop the bus!' her master cried. The few passengers looked up, hunched in their parochial reserve; but the driver, a turbaned Bengali alert to any crisis, stamped on his brakes. With a swirl of dust they slewed across the verge.

'Just what is going on? Look here, my dusky friend, you'd better have very good reason.' The driver advanced on Malibongwe.

'See, Anna, that field full of herbs! There's dandelion, there's feverfew, there's comfrey, there's – there's masses of the stuff. Come on, it's harvest time.'

'I don't believe it,' the driver muttered. Then, 'All right mate, you've got it coming.'

He crashed his gears. He lurched his bus back onto the road with a flurry of gravel. Poised at the door, our two botanisers were tossed headlong into gorse and keck.

Across the meadow, through a blackthorn hedge, a ring of stones beckoned to the pair. The Rollright Stones are a perfect double circle, not much more than a metre high, and they get up in the dark and dance. They glowed now with eldritch light. As Malibongwe and Anna stood in wonder, a mist, a miasma, gathered in the centre. The sun turned faint orange behind the gathering clouds. Light like soup flowed around them, grey-green, golden here and there, opaque yet revealing of another world. The bent trees, the sparse hedges, thickened and became intense. Shadows flickered among the boughs. The ground heaved, messy of mud, clay, roots and matter. Something manifested there before them: a thing of earth and rotting leaves, blackthorn and whitethorn, alder and hazel rooted and twining in its being. A kind of man, knotted, huge and massy, but in its hair twined elderberries, and hawthorn blossom, valerian flowers, and tiny peony, wild lobelia and oxalis. It opened its great yaw, or orifice of the massy head, its mouth of mud and moss. 'Eorgh!' it seemed to say, and 'Arugh!' and 'Harr!'

It spat earth; it made the sounds of trees in growth, amplified by many times, the sounds of roots and worms working in the loam, of rings of trees laid down through centuries of slow sleep. The grind of stone grating on stone, the ring of adze on wood, chisel on clunch, slate, the hoof that sparks on pebbles. Water tumbling through a rill, creaking millwheel, pike and hawk and fox and shrew, fire darting in the hearth, sounds making the ancient shire, tooth and tongue and slubbery chords tuned from years of slumber, speech coming slowly:

'Aargh! Ye! Forked things thinking, black beings, ye have thought me from my thick sleep, sithen siege, within wood; what would ye now with Wodwo green?'

'Hau! *Intokoloshe!* Run, Anna!'

But there was no escape. The green man filled all the space around them. He stank of bog, of deep fen-mud, he gave off a blend of the smells of earth and both dead and growing things.

'Er, um.' Brave Anna found her voice. 'We are South Africans. We are on a quest, O Wodwo, sir. We seek the tooth of Raka, Wise Man of aBaSotho. Like a Druid, sort of, if you get my drift. *Ja-nee? Nê?*' And then in simple words she explained the nature of their quest.

Strange affinity; perhaps not so strange. The threesome headed to the woods, the Wodwo gently parting undergrowth and boughs to let his new companions through. Every patch of earth has its beings, whether in Lusikisiki or in Little Norton; it is only the layering of language that differs. And the Wodwo struggled to find language after centuries of sleep. His woody discourse probed through epochs of English, parsing the speech as one parts the hair of a dog to seek out fleas, or the forest thickets for fruits and berries.

'Ethiop wights, eh, Blackamoors, eh? Am I your master then? How works this thing? Or am I your humble servant, bent to do your will? Nay, but ye be swart friends of Robin in the greenwoods. From Afric sands to my dear fields and woods. Come, little sooterkins, ride on my wide shoulders. We shall find your tooth.'

They jolted along on the giant's back, his knotted frame as hard as a disselboom. 'If only the ones in my women's group could see me now,' thought the Subaltern as she clung to ivy tendrils at his neck. The Wodwo's great club forged a path before them, and Malibongwe grinned and ducked as the saplings whipped by.

Where cheap reason dulls the mind, Wodwos go to sleep, unwanted, unknown, forgotten. Where the shaman's gift throbs, there such beings wake. An Orpheus in this, Malibongwe had the powers to animate the ones that take their being from dreams and deep earth. Unspelt, outside modern grammar, falling between the vocables and the particles, the signifiers and the signifieds of our dry-tongued articulation of the world, they lie dormant until the shaman comes.

And thus the shaman came to Sibford Gower.

The pony club was gathered on the village green. The wife of the Lord Lieutenant of the County handed out rosettes for dressage. Shandy-Smith and Bullock-Bentinck polished the bonnets of their vintage Bentleys. In the glorious light of a long summer dusk, the little Cotswold village glowed with ancient stone and new money. The London crowd lounged beside the door of the

Goat and Compasses, laconic, trendy. Polite applause as Emma, Sarah, Kate and Kimberley bore off their trophies. The Morris Dance and Cotswold Heritage Society tripped onto the green and waved their hankies, set their bells a-ringing.

'Saw two blacks in the Banbury bus this morning, do you know? Thought they kept to Brixton and such places.'

'Yairs. Gawd. And the driver is a Paki. Thought they kept to Bradford, haw haw.'

'Girton-Grope's boy's got himself a place in Cape Town. They go for next to nothing, bought himself a wine farm for the price of a flat in town.'

'Yairs. New empire, what? Recolonise the blighters. Chin chin.'

Up the lane, brushing against Volvos, SAABs and Aston-Martins, came the Wodwo and its friends.

Amid screams the village green emptied, flasks and bottles and picnic baskets abandoned on the grass. Morris dancers and ponies scattered. The Oldest Inhabitant rose from his bench and downed his Speckled Hen, waved his tankard in glee.

'The Manor House, my man,' Malibongwe cried down to him; and thus, in a cloud of black shag, the earth-ancient, Malibongwe and the Subaltern were led to the mellow home of the late Frank Lascelles, pageant-master of Empire, honorary chief of the Iroquois and the BaSotho.

'Should we knock?'

But the Wodwo wandered through the roses and straight into the door, splintered oak hanging from the hinges.

'Is there anybody home?' the travellers called.

No answer, for all of Sibford Gower was already gone. The lanes to Banbury were thick with flight.

With care Malibongwe and Anna searched the rambling house. It was a place of fantasy and charm with many curious things, objets de vertu, exotic gifts, antiques. A simulated Great Hall with a minstrel gallery, a Tudor tower built in 1920,

blackened oak panels, a stained-glass copy of Holman Hunt's 'The Light of the World' made into the study window. A statuette of Orpheus stood beside the entrance door, and lines of verse and much-loved hymns were carved into the hearth-beams.

'I like this place', said Malibongwe. 'Lascelles was a connoisseur. This *khaya*'s alive.'

'Dated, *liefling*, dated,' sniffed Anna. 'Here! *Kyk mos!* A silver casket!'

Trembling, they turned the silver key. And lo! On velvet lay the tooth of Raka.

'Is that it? Looks a bit greenish.'

'Anna. This is *diretlo*, strong Sotho *muti*. This is no common tooth. *Yiza moya!*' Soft but stern, Malibongwe spoke the words of awe.

Posting over shires in the late summer dusk, the Wodwo bore his happy pair through woods and dales, down the long hills of the Vale of Aylesbury, following the winding Thames past nunnery and Norman tower, past lock and weir, through field and fold with huddled flocks, keeping clear of habitation until through cunning ways, the ley lines of the olden people, they were brought up short by the security perimeter of Heathrow.

'Now be gone, my friends. This world be your'n, na mine.'

So saying, the Wodwo turned and vanished into gloam.

'*Sala kakuhle*, friend Wodwo green! *Enkos'!* I thank you from my heart!'

Would they ever meet the kind green man again? Malibongwe took Anna's hand and they made their way, with as much dignity as they could, up the long path round the hard perimeter, Boeings bearing down like lighted dragons in the dark.

'Ooh, *Jirre*, I'll be glad to be back home,' said Anna.

'So will this tooth, my friend. So will this tooth. *Mayibuye i'Afrika!* Don't look back, my dear Eurydice. We fly south.'